SYSTEMA PARADOXA

ACCOUNTS OF CRYPTOZOOLOGICAL IMPORT

VOLUME 15
INVASIVE SPECIES
A TALE OF THE LIZARDMAN OF SCAPE ORE SWAMP

AS ACCOUNTED BY HILDY SILVERMAN

NEOPARADOXA
Pennsville, NJ
2023

PUBLISHED BY
NeoParadoxa
A division of eSpec Books
PO Box 242
Pennsville, NJ 08070
www.especbooks.com

ISBN: 978-1-949691-27-6
ISBN (ebook): 978-1-949691-26-9

Interior Design: Danielle McPhail
www.sidhenadaire.com

Cover Art: Jason Whitley
Cover Design: Mike and Danielle McPhail, McP Digital Graphics
Interior Illustration: Jason Whitley

Copyediting: Greg Schauer and John L. French

DEDICATION

TO MY CHILD, WINTER, MY WHOLE HEART.

CHAPTER ONE

The lizard man had no name, but he did have desires. Hunger, mostly, but also warmth, sleep, and above all else, to be left alone in his home, South Carolina's Scape Ore Swamp. Other desires swept over him periodically, to which he would devote his entire self until they were fulfilled, he lost interest, or both. The only time they troubled him was when they were denied. Upon these fortunately infrequent occurrences, he reacted as one does when one's higher thought processes are underdeveloped — by flying into a rage.

The lizard man (let's just call him Stan, shall we? Even the basest creatures deserve names) had a scant sense of time and little self-awareness. At no point did he lie across his favorite sunning rock and wonder about his place in the world or how he came to be in it. He awoke to himself one day fully formed without memories of childhood or parents or origin of any sort and no desire to find out about any of it. All Stan knew was his hot, boggy, buggy swamp — where to find food, where to sleep safely so he didn't become food, and how to hide from the Unscaled.

The Unscaled (aka humans) eventually became more difficult to avoid. Of course, Stan had no way of knowing why, but the fault was mostly his own.

It all started one evening when a group of Unscaled visitors to Scape Ore Swamp left scraps behind at their campsite, which Stan sampled upon their departure. He spat out most of what he tried, except for what he found stuck along the insides of a small can. These soft little ovoids triggered a pleasurable response like he had never experienced before. They were so delicious they made him angry, and he spent the next hour running in a circle, pausing only to gouge trees with his claws and hiss at other swamp creatures that wisely fled in the opposite direction from his glowing, red eyes.

After a while, Stan's lizard brain was able to process the new input as desirable and therefore an experience he wanted to repeat. But the tasty, soft ovoids (we know them as butter beans) were gone, and though he spent the remainder of the night searching, he could not find more. It was then the man part of the lizard man's brain—what there was of it—assembled the available facts into a plan:

Unscaled have tasty-softs.

Unscaled live outside swamp.

Must leave swamp to find more tasty-softs.

Stan had to sit for several minutes, head aching from such unaccustomedly complex thought. However, when his mind returned to its usual want/need/take level of processing, he set off on his quest.

Using his exquisite sense of smell and sharp eyesight, he began tracking the path of the Unscaled who had left behind his newfound desire. His forked tongue flicked as he trekked through the swamp until it caught the campers' scent. He spotted their footprints in the muck, leading to the rough trail they had followed into and then out of Scape Ore.

Flicking and following, Stan came across a different set of tracks (left by the overinflated tires of an off-road vehicle). After a moment's hesitation at leaving the familiarity of his swampy home, Stan ventured off in the direction of those tracks, accompanied only by the moonlight, the chirps of crickets, and the peeps of amphibians.

Stan spotted a youthful Unscaled beside what he could only process as a large, possibly dead creature alien to his swamp. He had heard these beasts roaring past his domain, disturbing his hunts and his naps, and while he didn't understand what they were, he hated them.

The youthful Unscaled uttered sounds of unhappiness as he removed one of the carcass's ragged and flattened round legs and replaced it with another firm and whole. While watching, Stan realized this Unscaled might possess tasty-softs.

Now all the locals know this story from the perspective of seventeen-year-old Christopher, who had the misfortune of having a tire blow out while traveling the road past Scape Ore. The way he tells it, he heard a thump, looked up, and screamed as he beheld a seven-foot-tall lizard man with glowing red eyes charging toward him. At which point, he made the wise decision to dive into his car and drive away as fast as possible.

However, Christopher didn't know that when Stan had a desire, he would not let a simple thing like a fleeing noise-beast thwart him. Instead, he leapt onto the roof of the vehicle and began clawing it apart to scoop out the Unscaled within. His theory was simple — if the previous Unscaleds came with tasty-softs, then so must all. Therefore, if he acquired this one, his desire would be satisfied.

Stan was not a cruel or evil being any more than a hungry alligator or ravenous shark is. He did not desire Christopher's fear or pain or death. He simply did not care if those things occurred while satisfying his urge.

Fortunately for Christopher, the rest of his car was in better shape than his tire. Driving and screaming and perhaps expelling a bit of urine (as we can only speculate), he swerved and sped up to dislodge the lizard man clinging to his vehicle. He heard the screech of metal being stripped from his roof and the hissing of the monster attempting to claw its way inside.

Finally, the noise-beast's incredible speed and juddering gait overwhelmed Stan. His claws lost purchase and he tumbled off its back to roll, hissing and whimpering, across the unforgiving ground.

Enraged, bruised, and unfulfilled, Stan retreated to the safety of his swampy home. There he licked his wounds with flicks of his tongue and experienced the rare consideration that perhaps his desire was not worth it.

Unfortunately, Stan's desires were not so easily suppressed, not even by his survival instincts. It wasn't long before he again ventured out of his swamp along the path where the noise-beasts roamed. He was a bit more cautious this time. He also went a bit farther than his unfortunate first encounter with the runaway Unscaled until he caught the scent of his prey.

Stan discovered a small structure made of trees near the outskirts of what he didn't know (but we do) was the town of Bishopville. And within that structure (Elmore's Butter Bean Shed), he found his treasure — a stash of tasty-softs. With a hiss of sheer delight, he made quick work of the shed's door and then spent a delicious hour or so fulfilling his desire.

Sated, he retreated to his swamp. It was a slow and uncomfortable walk with a tummy full of tasty-softs, but Stan relished his triumph.

Now that his senses were keyed to the shed's location, he assumed he would have unfettered access to the treats forever.

Stan ducked behind trees to avoid the occasional passage of noise-beasts, which made his already lengthy six-odd mile shlep back to Scape Ore Swamp even longer. As he went, he reviewed his recent memories:

Rode a noise-beast.

Noise-beast moved fast.

Bucked off noise-beast.

Was farther down path.

This was followed by a thought:

Riding noise-beast faster than walking to tasty-softs.

This revelation made Stan growl and hiss, which roughly translated to, "Hell, yeah!"

Stan had no idea that he was sowing the butter beans of his own doom. Thanks to poor Christopher's frequent retelling of their 1988 encounter and subsequent reports of severe vehicular damage attributed to a seven-foot-tall scaly hitchhiker, Stan went from being a lizard man to the Lizard Man. As his fame grew, so did the opportunities to exploit his burgeoning legend, leading the folks in Bishopville and its surroundings to capitalize on the profitable side effect of his escapades — tourism.

This was why, by the twenty-first century, the hardy and long-lived Stan found himself a virtual prisoner in his own swamp, spending most of his days hiding from Unscaled, who showed up in droves.

His initial instinct was to fear them, assuming they intended to kill and eat him (as a predator himself, that seemed reasonable). However, as time passed, he found them more nuisance than threat, as they merely pointed and shouted on the rare occasions they spotted him. Many held up square objects that flashed irritating lights.

After years of dodging these Unscaled invaders, he sank into despair. His hisses and roars were met with cheers and fist pumps. Even charging only scattered them briefly, and his survival instincts prevented him from tearing them limb from limb due to their far greater numbers. Worst of all, his opportunities to visit the sacred shack of tasty-soft goodness were severely curtailed by the Unscaled, who always seemed to be waiting for him there.

Then, very late one night, when he was finally able to return to the shed, Stan made a horrifying discovery: it no longer contained tasty-softs (because the owner had converted it into something far more lucrative — a museum dedicated to the Lizard Man). Overwhelmed by disappointment, Stan reacted as simple beings with thwarted desires often do — by rampaging.

He smashed and clawed and tail-thwapped the museum's contents until nothing was left to destroy. Then he stormed back toward his swamp, only pausing along the way to savage a few late-night noise-beasts traveling past. The terrified screams of the Unscaled within their bellies were soothing... right up until one pulled over and got out with something other than a flashing square in hand.

This object barked, and Stan felt pain along his right arm. Looking down, he saw liquid he knew belonged inside him dripping down the outside. He tried to raise his arm to lick the wound, but that only made it hurt worse. Meanwhile, the Unscaled was shouting and slowly approaching with the barking thing pointed at him.

Stan rapidly figured out the following:

Unscaled pointed thing at me.

Thing barked.

Arm hurt and leaked.

Should avoid bark-hurts.

Stan roared and sprinted into the nearby woods. He kept running until satisfied that he had eluded the dangerous Unscaled. Then he spent the remainder of the night rolling in a mud patch to ease the pain in his arm and hissing at a world that had deprived him of his desired snack food and quiet, solitary existence.

Being a lizard man governed mostly by a lizard brain, the concept of being the author of his own woes never crossed Stan's mind. However, what did occur was that it might be time to find a new swamp, far from the invading Unscaled and their noise-beasts and flashing squares and bark-hurts.

And so, Stan set off on his quest to find a new, more private home. Perhaps (dare he hope?) one located near a new source of tasty-softs.

CHAPTER TWO

As the Lizard Man began his travels up Route I-77 (as confirmed by multiple reports of a roof-surfing, vehicle-gouging, giant lizard), a half-woman, half-wildcat called many things by many peoples crouched at the top of a hill in an isolated area of West Virginia's Preston County observing a skinny child of about six picking wildflowers. The sun had just begun to sink behind the nearby foothills, transforming the cloudless blue summer sky into a palette of purples ranging from the palest orchid to deepest indigo.

This woman-cat was untroubled by the ebbing sun. In fact, the darker it became the sharper her sight. This was not surprising, as most cats and catlike creatures enjoy excellent night vision. Especially the predatory sort.

However, the same could not be said for the child (Suzy Anne by name) who held the creature's attention. Glancing up and realizing how late it was getting, Suzy Anne began dashing toward home with her scrawny little arms wrapped tightly around her bounty of plucked flowers. Several escaped leaving a petal-strewn path for the creature, now fully manifested as a far larger-than-average mountain lion, skulking a short distance behind.

Suzy Anne paused and glanced over her shoulder. For just a moment, she caught sight of a furry shape as it slipped behind a small copse of trees. Something primal and wise within little Suzy Anne stirred, filling her belly with flutters and spurring her to run much faster toward her isolated, ramshackle house.

The giant cat followed, sometimes on two legs, sometimes on four. She felt no need to rush. Her mission that night was straightforward — observe, follow, and, if the moment presented itself, act.

Suzy Anne hopped up the two front steps to the tiny porch of the clapboard ranch she called home. As she fumbled around her bouquet for the front-door latch, the door flew open and nearly knocked her over.

The lionesque creature settled down in the tall weeds of the untended yard and observed the scene through bright, golden eyes.

"Mamma." Suzy Anne offered up her flowers to the figure looming in the threshold. "Lookit what I…"

"Where you been? Huh? Answer me!" A woman with a lined, leathery face more suited to someone twenty years older than her actual age stepped out and planted her hands on her ample hips. "You know you ain't s'posed to be out after dark, missy!"

Suzy Anne stammered, "B… but it's still a little light."

"You contradictin' me, girl?" Mamma took a step closer to Suzy Anne, voice dropping in that way that is so much more frightening to children than shouting.

Suzy Anne thrust her bouquet forward like a shield. "I picked these for you."

Mamma snatched the wildflowers from her outstretched hands. "And what was you supposin' I should do with a bunch of bug-filled weeds?" She chucked them over the side of the porch.

The cat growled deep within her chest. Her resolve solidified; she had made the right decision in choosing this particular prey.

Suzy Anne's lower lip trembled, and her wide blue eyes glistened as she gazed down at her discarded posies. "I just wanted to give you somethin' pretty. You always say there ain't been no pretty in your life."

Mamma shoved Suzy Anne, who stumbled back against one of the splintering wooden supports for the porch's overhang. "There surely hasn't. Not a one, 'specially not my ungrateful brat of a kid. Showin' up late, totin' a buncha ugly weeds, like that's gonna get her outta trouble for not mindin' me." Mamma jabbed a finger at the stoop. "You can just sleep out here tonight since you like it so much. Set yourself down on this step and you best be here when I get back. God help you if your spoiled little ass ain't right exactly here when I return!"

Suzy Anne sniffled and wiped her eyes with one pollen-stained fist. "Yes'm." She sat down, wincing at the newest pain in her back.

Mamma marched down the stairs and followed a trail of rock pavers barely visible beneath overgrown weeds behind the small house, muttering under her breath about burdens and regrets. She went to a tiny shed and yanked open the door, vanished inside for a moment, then came out with a large bottle of clear liquid in an unlabeled glass jug. She took a generous pull off the bottle and wiped her forearm across her mouth, closing her eyes with a deeply satisfied sigh.

When she opened them again, she found herself face-to-face with a nightmare.

A huge mountain lion, fur tawny in the rising moonlight, stood on its hind legs staring at her with a wholly unnerving combination of keen intelligence, contempt — and hunger.

"W…wam… wamp…" The bottle slid from Mamma's grasp and struck the ground with a dull clunk. Her mouth opened to release a scream of primordial fear.

The enormous cat opened her mouth, too — but much wider. She lunged and clamped her jaws around the mother's head. She worried it back and forth until she heard the satisfying crack of separating vertebrae. Hot blood filled her mouth, coursed down her throat, and inflamed her senses. The now-headless body collapsed, and she fell atop it.

After, when there was nothing recognizable left, the cat rocked back on her haunches and licked her bloodstained claws. She made her way around the front of the house, starting on four legs and then rising to two as she murmured ancient words to initiate what her kind called the Shift. She chose the appearance of a woman roughly the age of her dinner, figuring that under these circumstances, it would be more comforting than the form of a maiden or crone.

Suzy Anne flinched and looked up at the sound of what she thought was her mother's return. Instead, she was startled to see a tall, lean, and vaguely familiar woman with long, lustrous yellow-brown hair draped across her otherwise bare shoulders and breasts like a cloak.

"Hi'dy," Suzy Anne said uncertainly. "Say, ain't you the gov'mint lady who comes callin' time to time? 'Cept you usually got clothes on." She wasn't sure what a gov'mint was — it sounded like some sort of candy — but that's what Mamma had said sent this woman. Whatever it meant, her appearances at their door sure did make Mamma mad, and when she got mad, she blamed Suzy Anne. And when she got blamed… Suzy Anne began casting her gaze about nervously.

"Don't you worry, darlin'. Your time with her is done." The gov-'mint woman didn't smile, but her expression was gentle. "You're comin' with me tonight."

The woman had wide eyes that tilted up at the far corners and irises that shimmered bright gold like Suzy Anne imagined a fairy's would. She couldn't look away from them. "But Mamma said I got to wait for her or else." She pointed toward the back of her house, even though her arm suddenly felt too heavy to lift.

"What if I told you that you don't have to live in fear of her no more?" The woman's voice was soft, with a gentle hum underlying it that reminded Suzy Anne of a purring cat. She felt warm and safe in a way she couldn't remember ever feeling. So much so that she said, "I'd like that a whole lot. I hate that mean ol' witch."

The woman threw back her head and laughed. The moonlight set her gold eyes ablaze while shadows made it appear fangs filled her open mouth.

"You are so pretty." Suzy Anne swayed. She felt mushy inside from a rush of feelings for this strange woman that was beyond her understanding but powerful, nonetheless.

"So are you." The woman held out her hand. Her fingers were all the same length and tipped with nails so long the ends curved downward. Some were crusted with something reddish-brown, the sight of which made Suzy Anne's belly hitch. "Let's go."

Suzy Anne knew she shouldn't leave home with someone who was mostly a stranger and naked to boot. But the more she stared into this extraordinary woman's glowing golden eyes, the less worried she was about disobeying… who again?

The woman's hand curled around Suzy Anne's. As if in a dream, where actions have no consequences, the girl accompanied the wildcat who walked as a woman into the night.

CHAPTER THREE

Not surprisingly, Stan's migration north caught the attention of a few people. Which, again, was almost entirely on him, as he preferred car surfing his way out of South Carolina to the slow and exhausting alternative of walking.

He preferred traveling at night to better avoid detection, which meant he had fewer vehicles to choose from, particularly along more rural stretches of roadway. He finally spied a passing large noise-beast (A Ford Super Duty pick-up) with a nice, mostly empty back, which he managed to leap into when it slowed to avoid a possum crossing the road.

The ride went smoothly until the driver (an unfortunate fellow named Carl) arrived home and pulled into the driveway. Carl went to offload the new lawnmower he'd purchased... and found himself face to scaly face with a monster straight out of a 1970s creature double-feature.

Stan was just as displeased since he had been dozing rather peace-fully up until then. The Unscaled's holler jolted him awake, and he did what most startled predators would—lashed out with thick, sharp claws.

Carl's hands flew up reflexively to protect his neck and face and discovered fleshy trenches rapidly filling with blood. Backpedaling away from his Ford full of towering, roaring monster, Carl screamed. His neighbors' lights flashed on as they wondered who could be causing such a ruckus.

Stan leapt off the truck and ran down the street. He knew lights meant attention, and the last thing he needed was more of that. He pounded asphalt until he spied a passing noise-beast (a Porsche Panamera) and catapulted himself onto its roof.

The occupant and her friends were young, drunk, and in a hurry, so they ignored the whomp of a half-man, half-lizard landing on their roof in favor of turning up the volume on the car radio. They and their uninvited hitcher traveled for a decently long while until the inevitable happened.

The young lady driving, one Miss Claudine Beauchamp, sped past a state trooper who (due to a spat with a superior officer) had been put on graveyard duty monitoring a rural stretch just outside Charlotte, North Carolina. The trooper, Dillon Wakefield, pulled out in pursuit of Miss Claudine when his radar gun clocked her going twenty-five miles over the speed limit. However, as he caught up to the arrest-me-red Porche, he spied something on the roof that made him wonder if he'd dozed off and was only dreaming this pursuit.

Stan glanced over his shoulder at the whoop-whoop sound coming from behind his ride. Flashing blue lights stung his eyes. Whatever version of cusswords he had in his unique vocabulary of hisses and roars, he uttered them all.

Trooper Wakefield reached for his radio and reported, "...a big sum'bitch wearin' some kinda leathery outfit holdin' onto the roof of a Porsche goin' ninety." He had no idea how the hell the guy was clinging to the car at that speed, but there was surely no good reason for doing so.

Meanwhile, Claudine spotted the lights, heard the siren, and muttered, "Aw, shit, it's the po-po." The three underage passengers echoed her dismay. One in the back, Emily (more about her later), took a bottle they'd been passing and stashed it under the front passenger's seat, then opened her purse and hastily passed gum to the driver. Claudine pulled over onto the shoulder, put on her best smile (praying the minty gum would cover her Jack Daniels-scented breath), and rolled down the window.

Trooper Wakefield pulled over a cautious distance behind the Porsche, slid out of his vehicle, and drew his Sig Sauer pistol. Pointing it at the figure atop the car, he shouted, "Don't you move, boy, or you'll regret it!"

Claudine had been expecting the usual request to show her license and registration, followed by a quick conversation during which she'd play dumb and smile a lot and charm her way out of yet another ticket. So, when she saw the state trooper approaching with his gun drawn, her heart cartwheeled into her throat. Sticking her head out her window, the puzzled Claudine called, "I am sooooo sorry, officer. Did I do some little thang wrong?"

Meanwhile, the Lizard Man drew his legs up under himself and rose to a half-kneel, half-crouch on the sedan's roof. Trooper Wakefield froze, mouth gawping below his thick mustache. The earliest rays of dawn ignited the giant's... no, not a leather jacket, scales, with iridescence. Its eyes glowed red and baleful.

"What in the Holy Name of baby Jesus...?!" Trooper Wakefield squeezed the trigger.

Fortunately for Stan, he remembered all-too-well his previous encounter with an Unscaled using a bark-hurt. His arm still ached on occasion from that wound. So, as soon as he saw this one take aim, he hissed and sprang, thrusting with both three-fingered, claw-tipped hands and unhinging his jaw. At this point, three things happened almost simultaneously:

Claudine screamed in terror that a cop was shooting at her over a little speeding.

Bullets whizzed past the Lizard Man's head, missing it by inches.

Stan landed on the Unscaled, knocking him flat and sending the bark-hurt skittering away into the scrub brush along the road's shoulder.

Stan, who'd just plain had enough of constantly having his rides interrupted by screaming Unscaled, chomped down on the face wailing in abject horror just below his. He had never consumed Unscaled flesh, but it turned out it wasn't the worst thing he'd ever ingested (except for the furry bit around the mouth, which tickled his throat unpleasantly). While not nearly as good as tasty-softs, it was almost as palatable as the occasional wild pig he'd enjoyed back in his swamp.

Trooper Wakefield did what any human would after having his face bitten off. He died.

Stan scampered off into the woods, swallowing face and hissing over how poorly his travels were going.

After watching this horror unfold, Claudine screamed like a Fifties B-movie heroine on bath salts. She hit the gas and sped off, rapidly exceeding 100 MPH. There were no other unfortunately scheduled state troopers on duty, so they made it to the border of Virginia without further incident...

...until the combination of alcohol, speed, and panic-fueled adrenaline caused Claudine to lose control, spin out, and wrap the Porsche around a sizable maple tree.

Not surprisingly, the whole incident made the news, which drew the attention of the authorities — some of whom were less official but far more invested in keeping Stan's public escapades private.

CHAPTER FOUR

She called herself Eva Cather these days because humans insisted on using names, and she chose to live among them even though she had not been one of them for nearly a century. The other name for her kind was ridiculous and frankly insulting, as the dictionary defined wampus as "a strange, objectionable, or monstrous person or thing."

Sith cat, matagot, bakaneko—none of them or the legends attached to them quite fit the reality. Their species was simply too ancient, too beyond human comprehension, and (mostly) too careful at preventing their true nature from being revealed. To a host of human cultures in Asia, Europe, and Indigenous and rural America, those who could Shift were mostly legends to be feared by children and dismissed by adults.

True, some of her adoptive ancestors had behaved in monstrous ways, particularly the natural-born cat Shifters with a taste for human offspring. Her cat-side understood, given the tender sweetness of un-spoiled flesh. However, recent generations were more in touch with their human sides and thus rejected eating the young, much as some humans drew the line at consuming veal and lamb.

So much had changed over generations. Eva didn't dwell in an Appalachian cave but rather in a modestly furnished white Ranch-style home on the outskirts of Elkins, West Virginia. She had bills to pay and neighbors to avoid, just like everyone else. She kept in touch with her kind via a private Facebook Group with the unremarkable name of Cat Chat. And she worked for the Child Welfare Services Department investigating reports of abuse. It was a career that she was so passion-ate about she had practiced it through two iterations of her identity—nearly forty years.

There was a fundamental difference between how she and her colleagues managed investigations, though: Eva solved hers.

Not every circumstance warranted this decisive approach. Some involved parents whose wrongful actions could still be mitigated with therapy and coaching. But those who refused help, who rejected warnings to change, who reveled in tormenting their young physically and emotionally… they were fair game.

She took a sip from a mug filled with more cream than tea and rocked in the antique rocking chair that belonged to her birth mother — the one item she'd held onto from her original life. She watched through her front bay window as Suzy Anne swung on the tire swing. Eva had affixed it to a thick tree limb for the first child whose case she'd solved her way; the only one she'd ever considered keeping for her own. She idly wondered what became of him.

Eva was giving it a day before she brought Suzy Anne into the office to make sure the implanted memories of the previous night took. Her hypnotic abilities rarely failed, particularly with young children whose minds were so malleable. However, she had to be certain Suzy Anne only remembered her abusive, neglectful mother up and disappearing and her CWS guardian coming by for a welfare check and taking her to safety. The subsequent investigation would back up this sad and all-too-common tale.

No trace of the mother would ever be found (Eva had seen to that), and Suzy Anne would be placed with caring foster parents — who were also skilled at evaluating foundlings for worthiness to be inducted. If Suzy Anne fit the criteria, the couple would formally adopt her, train her in the Shift, and eventually induct her by blood ritual into becoming one of their kind. And if not, she would be given to a suitable human adoptive family. Either way, she'd have a far happier life thanks to Eva.

She picked up her cellphone and scrolled through the news. A headline caught her attention: Survivor of Tragic Auto Accident Shares Mysterious Tale of Lizard Man Attack. The subheader after she clicked through added: Driver and passengers allegedly heavily intoxicated. "Mystery solved," Eva smirked.

She rose and stretched with a purr, then opened the front door. "Suzy Anne! Come on in for lunch now."

Suzy Anne looked at her with half-open eyes. Her drowsiness was normal and would fade once the false memories were fully assimilated. "What'r we havin'?" she asked in a dreamy voice.

"Tomato sandwich," Eva answered. "Chips and a nice cold glass'a milk."

"Mmmm." Suzy Anne slid off the swing and stumbled toward the house.

Eva remembered her first meal after her new mother took her in—raw venison. It had been the early 1920s, when this region of the Americas consisted mostly of sorghum farmsteads and mines. Her birth father had died in a mining accident and her mother of scarlet fever, leaving her eleven-year-old self and six younger siblings in the care of their bitter grandmother, who thought parenting meant whupping children into mindless subservience.

One day Eva (then called Violet) wandered away from her remote holler home in pursuit of a large kitty she'd spied down the dirt road. She followed it, oblivious to the danger or perhaps uncaring since her sorry life was hardly worth preserving. Finally, the wildcat turned and confronted her with a rumbling growl. Even then, she didn't run but rather stood and stared, fascinated by the enormous creature's golden eyes that appeared lit from within.

The mountain lion had then done something so unexpected Eva could only gasp and clasp her hands beneath her chin. It rose onto its hind legs and slowly transformed into a woman about Mee-Maw's age.

The woman spoke in a thick accent Eva later learned was Scottish. "Are ye food or are ye bairn?"

She didn't understand the second word, but she certainly recognized the first and knew she didn't want to be that. She replied, "I'm a bayurn."

The old woman rubbed her chin. "Suppose we shall see 'bout that." Then she'd waved Eva toward the entrance of a cave. "C'mon then."

She had entered and did not leave for the remainder of her childhood. Within that den, she'd learned everything from the old woman who became her mother—the sacred utterances of the Shift, how to hunt, control minds, and hide in plain sight.

Upon her induction, she became part of an extended, if contradictory, family unit, one whose members rarely interacted beyond the age of maturity due to their highly territorial nature. They could love one another, but preferably from afar. Males and females came together to breed but typically parted after coupling. If a cub resulted (an event that even back then was uncommon), it remained with the mother only until it could Shift independently. It was a lonely existence, particularly for those who also eschewed living among humans, but also one of freedom and power.

Eva never regretted being chosen. The alternative would have been ongoing abuse and neglect ending in an early death, as befell her biological siblings. Other than taking her mother's rocker from the ramshackle porch of Mee-Maw's abandoned shack, Eva had never looked back. She was certain Suzy Anne, and all the other children she'd rescued, wouldn't either.

CHAPTER FIVE

Eva's intervention was not appreciated by all her foundlings.

His name was Daniel. That was all he retained from his original family thirty years after she took him. His current last name was Smith. He'd chosen it because it was a surname that belonged to so many people that it didn't really belong to anyone — much like himself.

Daniel began life as a child of poverty. His personal heritage was a mélange of the people who'd settled West Virginia — Cherokee, Black, Appalachian poor whites — and he was frequently reminded that he would never completely fit in with any of them.

His mother ran off when he was about four with 'some Northern rich boy,' or so his father told him. While her abandonment was willful, his father's subsequent neglect was unintentional. A coal miner since his late teens, his father's damaged lungs cost him his ability to work or take care of his only son. By the time he turned six, little Daniel was malnourished, wore clothes he'd outgrown two years previously, and tasked with his withering father's care.

The state finally took notice when he was never enrolled in grammar school. They sent Eva (calling herself Lora back then) to investigate, and a few months later, his father disappeared, never to be found. The authorities performed a cursory investigation but ultimately wrote it off as a weak man's decision to crawl off and die alone like some diseased animal.

The night he vanished, Daniel went to sleep on his mattress. He woke up in a comfortable bed in a tidy house he soon learned belonged to Lora, his new legal guardian.

Daniel only vaguely remembered his time at Lora's, and even those few memories were dreamlike. He recalled being treated with benign indifference — she fed him well, gave him clean clothes, got him medical care, and generally provided all the sustenance needed to transform him from rickety to robust. But he never felt at ease in her presence. In his murky recollections, she was benevolent but remote, attentive without affection, solicitous yet disturbing.

It wasn't until he turned seven that he had his next clear memory. Lora had hung a tire swing on the tree in front of her house, and he was swinging in the crisp autumn air. He remembered footsteps crunching through the piles of fallen leaves and turning his head to see Lora studying him with her strange gold eyes. The further the sun descended, the brighter they shone.

"I come to a decision, Danny," she said in her mountain folk accent.

"What 'bout?" He stopped pumping his legs until the swing slowed.

"I ain't meant to be a mother. I understand its purpose and benefits, but I lack the..." She waved her hand as if attempting to conjure up the rest of her sentence. Failing that, she shrugged. "You deserve better'n me. So, I am gonna give you over to foster folks better equipped to nurture you on a deeper level. You understand?"

Daniel felt sad that Lora was giving him away like a puppy that had failed to be more lovable than it was a nuisance. At the same time, he experienced a sense of relief and a stir of excitement. "I'm gettin' a new poppa?"

She nodded. "And a mamma, although y'need to understand that they won't stick 'round once they've raised you up. It's not the way of our kind to form long-term family units, but some don't mind livin' together peaceful-like for a stretch to bring up young'uns. Assumin' their evaluation of your potential results in that outcome."

He only understood part of what she was saying, so fixated instead on the thrill of getting a new family. He didn't know what he'd been missing at the time but later came to realize it was love.

Daniel was placed in the care of Willa Tatum and Aaron Miller, who resided in a cabin that backed onto the Potomac State Forest in Western Maryland. He recalled that time more clearly, and it was as happy a period as he ever knew. They might have shared the same odd golden irises and languid mannerisms as Lora, but he felt their affection. They were very encouraging and supportive during the years he lived with them... although they made him feel like he was being evaluated constantly. They would ask about his school day, but mostly to quiz him on his interactions with other children, particularly those who bullied him:

"How did you respond to that insult?"

"What would you have done if you could get away with it?"

He also sensed they were avoiding fully embracing him as their own. He worked hard to please them by getting good grades, behaving in school, and generally doing all the things he understood good boys were supposed to. Yet they remained — aloof.

When he turned twelve, they explained the time had come for him to demonstrate his worthiness. "We are going to show you our true selves, and you are going to join us," Ma Willa said. "We can extend our abilities to you only this once, so if you are unable to prove your potential, we will have to make… different arrangements." At least she had the decency to look downcast at the thought.

He felt like he'd been kicked in the gut. "But I don't want to leave. I love this house, and my room, and you — "

"Good." Pa Aaron rested his wide hand with its thick-nailed fingers that were all the same length on Daniel's shoulder. "Use that to motivate you. There are so few of us left… we want you to succeed."

The night itself remained emblazoned in Daniel's memory. It was an experience that could not be erased with their hypnotic talents. Which was why to even reach that point in the assessment process was considered a significant achievement, or so his foster parents insisted. They had to trust he was worthy of this ultimate test, knowing he would remember and could tell others if he so chose.

They told him how their kind survived in secrecy throughout the centuries. That they were on the wane, with few naturally born over the past couple of centuries, so those remaining decided to induct select humans still young and impressionable enough to learn their ways. They mentioned others, collectively referred to by humans as cryptids, some of which could also control their shifts between human-appearing and animal, while others remained combinations of both or entirely bestial.

Then Ma and Pa stripped naked and told him to do the same. He obeyed, fascinated and horrified in equal measure, and then drank the shot glass full of salty, crimson liquid they handed him. "The power's in the blood," Ma explained.

They chanted words in a language unlike any Daniel had ever heard; a combination of unrecognizable words and chest-deep rumbles and hisses. Then their bodies transformed. Limbs lengthened, haunches thickened, bellies sagged, and body hair sprouted. Their faces blurred and reformed into the visages of what he recognized as wildcats of some kind (his later researched confirmed they were cougars).

Then he was on fire.

He opened his mouth to scream, but only a weird yowling emerged. He felt his teeth grow long and sharp and watched as his fingernails did the same. His normally medium-brown skin vanished beneath a thick dark pelt. He fell forward and caught himself with forelegs instead of arms. His vertebrae felt like they were cracking apart as his spine stretched and his coccyx extended into a tail.

Abruptly, the agony vanished, and there he was, a giant cat facing two even larger. They bumped against his sides and nuzzled him before rising on their hind legs and leading him out the back door into their yard, which extended to meet the edge of the state forest. His foster parents had always warned him not to wander into those woods because there were creatures within that might gobble him up. Now they led him into their depths to do the gobbling.

It was the single most amazing experience of Daniel's life. Sensations of strength and stealth and freedom washed over him as he ran through the woods. He was never a particularly athletic child, but now he felt unlimited by shortness of breath or weary muscles. He could run for miles, forever, and he wanted to. He wanted to feel this powerful for the rest of his life!

Ma and Pa took turns demonstrating how to hunt, to corner, and then to strike. They communicated with him—that was the only way he could put it since they didn't use words or even vocalizations. His incredibly keen senses were completely attuned to theirs, so he just knew what they expected.

He gave it to them when he brought down a doe. A part of him watched aghast as he tore out the creature's throat, then ripped its warm corpse apart and devoured it—bones, pelt, and all. But the cat was in charge, and it felt no pity for the hapless deer nor questioned what felt like the most natural of acts.

Then his foster parents led him deeper into the woods. Within a blind sat a man, a hunter, shotgun across his lap, holding infrared binoculars to his eyes.

This man would steal our prey, Pa communicated. You will stop him.

His body, strong and feral and craving sustenance like he hadn't since he was a malnourished tot, wanted to obey and was as eager to rend the man's carcass as it had the doe's. But his mind, his human self, rebelled. He wasn't a killer, certainly not of some stranger who'd never done him wrong. The man might have a family, and they would miss him as Daniel did his father. What right did he have to inflict that pain on innocents simply because he'd been granted the power to do so?

He is prey. Ma communicated. We are predators. Claim your status in this world, and you can have this, be this, forever.

His heart ached. He knew this was the moment, the decision. Power or conscience, strength or empathy, dominance or mercy.

Daniel chose. He turned and slunk away. Behind him, he heard the disappointed yelps of his foster parents.

By the time he reached the border of their backyard, he was wholly human again. He heard a single gunshot followed by a scream. In the silence that ensued, his heart ached with the realization that his decision hadn't made a whit of difference. He had changed no one's destiny but his own.

The day after, a part of him clung to the hope that Ma and Pa might have come to love him so much that they would forgive his failure to prove worthy of their gift. But instead, they turned him out, saying only that "Other arrangements have been made" and wishing him safe travels down whatever mundane path his human life took.

Daniel spent the remainder of his youth being sent from one foster home to the next. Some were decent, others were horrible, but all were as temporary and forgettable as an overnight stay in a cheap roadside motel. None offered the promise of love and magic that life with Ma Willa and Pa Aaron had.

As a young man, he started acting out in small ways—petty theft, fistfights over insults and girls, and selling pot for a local dealer. His life probably would have taken a darker turn if, on the cusp of his aging out of the system, a mysterious organization hadn't recruited him before a local gang could. That organization, known as the Wranglers, was happy to find someone already aware of the reality of cryptids, and Daniel was equally pleased to find people who knew they were real. After years of study and training, they assigned him to his first and current charge— the Lizard Man of Scape Ore Swamp.

Emily Whiteside had been in the rear right seat when the accident occurred, and though she'd sustained multiple traumatic injuries, she was the only girl wearing her seatbelt. Emily had quite the story to share, and Daniel stood by her hospital bed, recording every painkiller-slurred word.

"We was just having a fun night, girls' night out, y'know? And then it got to being late, so we climbed back into Claudine's car, and was driving along home, and passing the bottle... um, of co-cola, and then the po... police guy, he pulled us over for some reason."

A very bored-looking deputy named Lucy Steele was also in the room, sent by the local sheriff's department to investigate the crash and its connection to a state trooper's horrific killing. She executed an epic eye roll at Daniel, who had led her to believe he was an insurance investigator. "The driver of their vehicle was speeding. A lot."

He ignored her. "Go on, Emily."

She sniffled. "It's all kinda jumbled in my mind, y'know? But all'a sudden, there's gunshots and Claudine's screaming, and we all start screaming 'cause we don't know what's happening, and then Claudine guns it outta there. And then... we hit something. I don't clearly recall anything else 'til I was here, and then they told me," she broke off with a sob, "they're all gone. Claudine, Becky, that two-faced Annabelle who had no business joining us, but whatever... all gone."

Daniel gave Emily a moment to cry it out. "In your initial statement, you said Claudine mentioned someone else at the scene. Can you tell me about that?"

Deputy Lucy chimed in, "Describe the attack on the trooper. Who did it?"

Daniel clenched his teeth until his jaw ached. He reminded himself that though his and the deputy's specific goals differed, their missions were intertwined. He couldn't overplay his authority, or Lucy might figure out he wasn't what he claimed.

Emily wiped her running nose and eyes with her cast-wrapped right hand. "I didn't see any actual killing, like I told them other officers. But Claudine, she must've, 'cause she kept repeating... I dunno, it was crazy... like oh, God, what is that, I think it's eating him, oh, Lord—"

"But did you personally see anything?" Daniel leaned in and patted Emily's unbroken hand gently. "You can tell me. I won't judge you."

He heard Deputy Lucy huff behind him and resisted the urge to glare over his shoulder. Emily blinked her wide, wet eyes and leaned closer. "I did look out the back when Claudine started caterwauling. It was dark, mind you, and I might've had a drink or two, but," she hesitated, "I saw it too. The monster."

"And can you describe it?"

Emily chewed her lower lip. "It was big. Like, way bigger than a regular man. And it was kinda… scaly. And, um, I think it had claws." She nodded, wincing within the cervical collar. "Yeah, it did. I saw when it raised its hand whilst on top of that cop."

"That's good, Emily, really good." He patted her hand again encouragingly. "Did you see anything else, its face, its eyes…?"

She shivered and shrank back against the bed. "That's right, that's the other thing Claudine kept ranting on. Glowing red eyes, she said." Emily looked up at him imploringly. "What in the hell was it?"

"Vodka and Jack," Lucy muttered. "So, your statement is the suspect who murdered Trooper Wakefield was a giant, scaly monster." She flipped her notepad closed. "Thank you so, so much for that." She headed for the door. "Mr. Smith, you coming?"

"I will be right behind you," he lied. She shrugged and walked out.

Returning his attention to Emily, Daniel said, "Thank you, you've been very helpful, Miss Emily. I hope you recover quickly." He took out his card and placed it on her bedside table. "Should you remember anything else about the creature you saw, you just give me a call or send an email." He tapped the card.

"I will." She raked her left hand through her disheveled, purple-streaked hair and sat up a bit straighter. Her thin hospital gown slid down, baring her collarbone and shoulder. "Um, did they give you my info? Y'know, in case you want to ask me… anything else?"

He pressed his lips into a thin smile. "Oh, I'm sure if I have any other questions, I'll be able to find you." He nodded politely, then turned to leave.

"Hey, you didn't answer my other question. Do you know what that thing was?"

He mulled over possible responses and decided to go with a partial truth. "I think it was something that had no business being on that road. It's up to me to figure out why he was there and where he's heading next before anyone else gets hurt."

Her eyes widened. "Uh, oh, wow. Okay then."

Once back in his Jeep, Daniel sat in the parking lot for some time, reviewing his notes from Emily. He compared them to the reports he'd collected from Carl and several other drivers about the Lizard Man, who was no longer in Scape Ore Swamp. By the time he'd plotted all the incidents and sightings on his smartphone's mapping app, he had a solid idea of where the creature might head next.

The Lizard Man was about to cross into the territory of someone who would be even less welcoming than ordinary humans, someone who the Wranglers had already been keeping a close eye on due to her possible connection to several disappearances in that region over the past four decades.

"God damnit," Daniel muttered. "This is going to be bad."

He set his GPS, peeled out of the parking lot toward Route I-77, and headed north to West Virginia.

CHAPTER SIX

It took Stan another night of hopping rides (literally) and skulking on foot to reach a potential new home. While it wasn't quite as hot and humid as he would have liked, the huge, wooded area at least somewhat resembled his swamp. There were lots of trees to hide behind, plenty of animals to stalk, and at least one large body of potable water.

Unfortunately, there were also frequent incursions by the Unscaled—hiking, swimming, and generally getting in Stan's way. But this new habitat was quite large, and over the next few days, Stan found plenty of places isolated enough that he could nap or hunt or take a dump in peace. So, he settled in and claimed this new not-quite-a-swamp-but-good-enough territory as his own.

Unfortunately, Stan never considered that someone else might already have a claim on this area. Eva couldn't survive on bad parents alone, so she frequently hunted the Monongahela State Forest for game. And while it was a vast territory, she had no interest in sharing it.

Daniel knew this about Lora (now Eva, he had to keep reminding himself) because he and the Wranglers kept close tabs on many of the known cryptids throughout the United States. They had to in order to keep the truth of their existence hidden—a full-time job for the teams spread across the country. The ones assigned to the various sasquatch tribes alone were run ragged because the big hairy folk were just so damned popular. It was important work, though, preserving the notion that these uncanny beings were merely figments of people's overactive imaginations. Otherwise, if their existence ever became accepted by the mainstream, humanity would do what it always did to strange and potentially threatening creatures and wipe them off the face of the Earth.

While the primary mission of the Wranglers was to preserve these beings by covering their tracks, they also made sure the cryptids didn't cross too many lines and endanger the public. Which was why Eva's suspected escapades kept her on the Wranglers' radar, as her occasional devouring of humans (even despicable ones) posed a threat in more ways than one. And now they also had Stan in their sights due to his violent road trip, capped off by the newsworthy slaughtering of a state trooper. While it would be unfortunate to lose the Lizard Man, who was the only known cryptid of his kind, or a cat wampus, given how few of them were left, if Stan and Eva's reckless behaviors couldn't be contained, the Wranglers were prepared to put them down.

Daniel knew this, and the possibility disturbed him deeply. Although he had seriously mixed feelings about Eva (being fairly certain, after reading the Wranglers' files on her after he joined up, that she had eaten his father), he realized she must have had at least some good intentions when she decided to remove him from a life of squalor and deprivation. He didn't have any personal ties to the Lizard Man, but the simple yet fascinating creature had been his assignment for the past twelve years. Daniel hated the thought of potentially being ordered to destroy him.

Speaking of Stan, he was blissfully unaware of the danger he'd put himself in through his recent adventures and choice of forest home. He had settled into his new life quickly. It was a bit chillier at night than he would have preferred, but not unmanageable. He hadn't located any tasty-softs but held out hope that he might yet stumble across a stash of the delectable treats. In the meantime, there were plenty of fresh critters to satisfy the carnivorous elements of his omnivore's appetite.

One evening, Stan passed through a dense section of woods on the trail of soft-scaled winged meat (a flock of wild turkeys). Wholly focused on sampling a new delicacy that traveled in a handy multipack, he flicked his forked tongue and followed their scent to a small clearing. But just as he was about to spring upon his prey, his tongue caught the scent of something else that brought him up short. From between two of the old-growth trees ringing the clearing across the way, Stan beheld the approach of a pair of glowing orbs.

Eva moved toward the small flock of wild turkeys on her hind legs, then dropped to all fours and readied herself to pounce. Abruptly, the fur along her spine bristled, a warning that another predator was close at hand. She cast her gaze around, expecting to see a bear or coyote, but instead spotted something with bright red eyes that absolutely, positively did not belong anywhere near her hunting grounds. She growled and stalked slowly into the clearing.

Though not the brightest of birds, the wild turkeys couldn't help but notice the approach of two monstrous predators. They reacted with loud squawking and a mad, wing-flapping dash toward an exit from the clearing not blocked by either a giant lizard or cat creature.

Stan turned and hissed at their tailfeathers. He briefly considered charging after them, but his annoyance over having his easy pickings chased off by another won out, so instead, he turned and glowered at the big, furry creature responsible. He had not seen a mountain lion in ages (they'd been rendered extinct in South Carolina about a hundred years prior), but he remembered them being a challenge during the few instances he had crossed paths with one. He stomped into the clearing and bellowed his displeasure.

But then the big cat did something he had never seen another creature do when confronting him—instead of turning tail and scampering off, this one snarled and charged straight at him. Then it did something even more unexpected by rearing up on its hind legs before slashing at his neck with extended claws. Stan was so startled he barely raised his scaled arms in time to block it from tearing out his throat.

The part of Eva that remained capable of rational thought wondered, What the hell is this thing, and why is it here? She knew there were other beings in the world besides humans and her kind, but they normally gave one another a wide berth. This creature was covered in scales and appeared to be a huge man-lizard—definitely not suited to her mountainous territory. Regardless, most of Eva was mountain lion, so she was less concerned with the whats and whys of her competition's presence and more focused on the kill-and-remove aspects.

Stan bellowed and smacked the cat, sending it yowling and tumbling across the clearing into a nearby oak. It staggered back onto all fours and shook its head in an oddly Unscaled-like way. The golden glow of its eyes dimmed briefly before flaring even brighter than before, and Stan read hatred in its snarling face. He raised his huge fists and strode toward it with the intent of pummeling the light out of its eyes permanently.

Eva shook off a monetary daze following her collision with the tree. Assessing that the huge lizard man's strength was at least equal to hers, she executed a feint by jumping at him and testing his reaction time.

Already in motion, Stan lurched awkwardly to avoid her as she landed at his left.

She followed up with a swipe at his leg. Her claws raked along his scales, but she barely scraped the surface. Nevertheless, his hiss and subsequent attempt to club her over the head indicated he'd felt it. Slow reflexes, armored, strong, she determined. Bringing him down would require an act of stealth, then, not force.

As their brutal dance progressed, Stan developed his own less sophisticated assessment of his opponent:

Cat fast,

Cat scratchy,

Cat tough,

Hate cat!

Caught up in their battle, neither Eva nor Stan caught a whiff of a third predator (of sorts) as he approached the clearing as quietly as possible.

Daniel had tracked Stan to the portion of the Monongahela State Forest near the North Carolina border days ago, but it had taken him some time to chart his cold-blooded target's path to this isolated area. Against the advice of Chief Moore, who oversaw Wrangler deployments from Maine down to Alabama (Florida being off-limits to the Wranglers, as they had their own cryptid management division—a publicly denied, state-government sanctioned operation based in Ochopee), he had ventured alone that night to where he believed he might catch the Lizard Man unawares and knock him out using a standard-issue tranquilizer gun. Daniel wasn't stupid; he knew he was taking a big risk going solo. But he also feared for his charge's continued existence if he didn't move quickly to subdue and remove him from Eva's territory before she found him.

It turned out he was too late for that. Daniel followed the sounds of a ruckus to a clearing and found the cat woman and the Lizard Man already locked in mortal combat.

He clutched his tranq gun and pondered the best course of action that would allow both cryptids to survive. Despite the emotions seeing Lora or Eva or whatever she was calling herself stirred up, he didn't want her destroyed any more than he wanted the subject of his years-long guardianship to perish. Both were highly endangered creatures, and Daniel firmly believed that they had the same right to exist as any living being.

Stan roared with frustration and pain, unable to subdue the fast-moving cat as it repeatedly darted in, slashed his flesh, and leapt away before he could land a blow. Spurred by his survival instinct, the man portion of his lizard man brain kicked his thought processes up a notch. He stopped swinging his claws through the space left in the furry fiend's swift wake and instead scanned the ground for a weapon. He spied a large broken branch nearby and jumped over to it.

Eva grumbled in satisfaction as the lizard man leapt toward the trees. She briefly debated pursuing and finishing him off, but she was tired and sore and so decided to be content with having driven him off. If he did not choose to vacate her hunting grounds permanently, well, then she would return when she was refreshed and end him. Dropping back to all fours, she started to turn away...

...just as Stan picked up the huge branch, sprang high into the air, and landed, already swinging the branch down at her head...

...at which point Daniel muttered, "God damnit!" He aimed and fired at the Lizard Man.

The situation deteriorated rapidly from there, at least for Eva and Stan. Eva caught sight of the giant lizard above her moments before the branch would have caved in her skull. She managed to whip her head aside but couldn't completely dodge the blow, which landed across her spine and ribs. She dropped to the ground with an agonized yowl.

Stan had less than a handful of seconds to relish her suffering. A sudden stinging sensation on the side of his neck became a warmth that flowed up and into his already battle-weary brain. The injured cat blurred, as did the woods around it, and he felt as though his body were submerged in mud that drew him down into a deep, dark pit from which he couldn't escape.

Daniel sucked in a breath and stood up. He holstered his tranq gun and cautiously entered the center of the clearing. The Lizard Man was lying on his side, forked tongue lolling into the dirt, red eyes almost entirely shut. Satisfied, he slowly approached the mountain lion crumpled on the ground across from her now-senseless foe.

"Lora," he said, deliberately meeting her dimly glowing golden gaze. He spread his fingers wide and held his hands palms up. "I'm not here to hurt you."

She half-raised her head, snarling and snapping her jaws in a warning to back off. But it was clear she couldn't do anything more. Her breathing was labored, likely from the ribs visibly caved in along her right side. Still, if he had any hope of aiding her, he needed her cooperation.

"Do you recognize me? Check my scent. It's Danny... Daniel Sizemore." His original full name sounded odd to his own ears.

Her nostrils flared. She blinked. Then she laid her head on the ground and whimpered.

Torn, Daniel glanced back at the Lizard Man. It was unlikely any natural predator would disturb him the rest of the night, and he appeared mostly uninjured from the fight. It would take some time for Daniel to get back to where he'd parked his Jeep and pull out the tarp, ropes, and other equipment necessary to haul the Lizard Man out of the woods and into the large cage he'd brought to stash him in. Peering closer at the wampus cat's wounds, he doubted she'd survive if he left her lying there, even given the accelerated healing abilities he knew her to possess.

Daniel made his choice.

He knelt beside the wounded cat's head. "Lora... Eva, I hear that's what you call yourself now. I want to get you out of here and treat your injuries. But I need you to Shift back. Can you do that?"

He sensed she was studying him, her intrinsically untrusting nature warring with her recognition that she needed help. "I swear I mean you no harm." To prove it, he bent closer to her mouth and exposed his throat.

She let out a chuff he took as acceptance. Then her mouth began to move around the utterances of the Shift. Just hearing them again after so many years sent a chill down Daniel's spine of combined longing and fear. He scooted back and watched.

Within moments the cat vanished, replaced by a battered, nude woman lying on the ground, her long, dark blonde hair fanned across her body. She gasped, and her striking gold eyes shone not from a preternatural inner light but with tears of pain. "D...Danny," she managed. "Wh... how are you..."

He shook his head. "We can talk later. Right now, I have to get you out of here." He shrugged off his jacket and draped it gingerly over her. "I'm going to be as careful as I can, but I'm afraid this will hurt."

Her jaw muscles clenched visibility, but she nodded. Daniel slid his arms under her knees and around her shoulders. He lifted her as flat as possible, but she still cried out in such agony that he winced. "Sorry, I'm sorry," he murmured repeatedly as he carried her through the densely wooded area back down the thin trail he'd blazed to the clearing. He did his best not to jostle her while still moving at a decent clip. Her increasingly labored breathing and moans spurred him along, worrying all the while that she wouldn't make it now that she was in her vulnerable human form.

"Danny." He looked down at her face, which though tense with pain, appeared younger than his recollections from childhood. The more he gazed at her, the clearer his memories of that time became, even though she herself didn't quite match them. Her facial features were slightly different—lips fuller, nose slimmer, and eyes a bit wider. Her hair used to be lighter, too, almost platinum, and it had been shorter.

"No… hospital," she continued. "Injuries… too much explanation. Know where… my house is?"

Even wounded, she was far too canny not to have figured out his timely appearance was no mere coincidence, so he didn't bother playing ignorant. "Yeah, I know. I'll take you there, don't worry."

She clenched her teeth tightly and managed a nod. Then, with a sigh, she fainted.

He made it back to the Jeep and carefully laid Eva across the back seat. As he drove toward her house—the place that had been his home for almost a year—emotions and memories churned deep inside him, making it hard to concentrate on the dark and twisting roads. He would have a lot to explain to Eva after she'd recovered enough to start demanding answers.

Fair enough. As far as he was concerned, she had a lot to answer for as well.

CHAPTER EIGHT

Eva shifted uncomfortably against the pillows propping her up in her Shaker sleigh bed, wincing at the shooting pain in her side. She still had some time before her ribs fully healed. She looked over at the young man sitting in the utilitarian wooden chair across from her and remembered those wide, dark brown eyes gazing up from the face of a small boy so many years ago. She very rarely encountered one of her rescues after she'd placed them with a foster family, save for the handful granted the gift of the Shift and even those she only occasionally communicated with through Cat Chat.

Her curiosity was piqued, but so was her innate distrust. It could not be a coincidence that Danny had returned, especially given the fortuitous timing of his arrival. She had a suspicion as to why, but his actions in bringing her home and taking care of her since the night before belied it.

She decided to take the direct approach. "What brings you back to my neck of the woods?"

"I didn't come for you," he snapped. Then he rubbed his jaw and sighed. "I wasn't looking for you, Lo… Eva. I was on the trail of the being that attacked you. The Lizard Man."

She grimaced, remembering the scaly monstrosity. "That what you call the big booger, hm? Kind of on the nose, ain't it."

Danny shrugged. "No one's ever come up with a better name."

She noticed that he no longer sounded like a local. She had done some work over the years to moderate her speech patterns with mixed results. Considering her original patois was so old and thick, even other native Appalachian folk didn't recognize some of the words she used. It had been a necessary evil to maintain her current persona. And that was before she'd chosen a field in which so-called educated people looked down their noses at anyone who sounded too much like a mountaineer.

"Where d'you wind up, boy? No offense, but you sound like a Northerner."

Danny shifted in his seat. "Yeah, well, I got handed off quite a bit after Willa and Aaron rejected me. Spent some time bouncing around New England during my formative years. I guess it took since I'm living in the South again, and my original accent hasn't come roaring back." He snorted. "Gotten called a Yank more than once."

Eva sensed his resentment when he said rejected. She could understand that. He had been shown the power of the Shift only to have it taken away forever. A shame; Danny had shown promise as a child. She wondered what he'd done wrong but decided not to poke that obvious sore spot.

Besides, she had a more pressing concern. "So, how'd you come to be responsible for this Lizard Man?" She fixed her attention on him, compelling a direct answer.

He immediately averted his gaze. "You don't have to do that. I knew I'd have to tell you the truth when I decided to help you. I'm... a member of an organization that sees to it cryptids like yourself and the Lizard Man stay safe and off humanity's radar."

"Ah." That confirmed her suspicions. "You mean the Wranglers."

Danny's eyes widened. "You know about us? How?"

She started to shrug but winced and pressed her injured side gingerly. "Can't speak for all pre-humans, but my kind has certainly been aware a network's come up over the years dedicated to covering our tracks. We've been appreciative of their efforts—for the most part."

His lips twisted into a wry grin. "What parts haven't you appreciated?"

"Ones when your compatriots responded to certain... let's call 'em missteps, by eliminating the one who messed up." She bared her teeth briefly. "Which is why we've made it our business to learn as much about your organization as possible."

Danny frowned. Clearly, the watcher didn't like knowing he was being watched in return. She sensed he wanted to demand answers as to how her kind had tracked his and gathered so much information. However, all he said was, "They took me in and gave me a direction and a purpose when I sorely needed both."

"And you told them all about us in return. About me." A wave of concern washed over her. Just how much of a threat did his reappearance in her life pose? Did the Wranglers know what she had been up to since she first took him in? Was it her turn to be disappeared?

"I told them what I knew, which frankly wasn't much," he replied. "It was enough for them to identify what you and your kind were and tell me about all the other cryptids in the world. The fully evolved ones and the less-so, like the Lizard Man."

He appeared to study her expression closely. "Like I said, I'm not here for you. You're the responsibility of someone else entirely. Because of our past connection, my superiors felt I had too personal a stake in cat wampuses to remain objective and effective."

She cringed, but not from pain this time. "Could you kindly not use the W word? It's rude."

"Rude, huh? You know what I find rude, Eva?" His voice dropped to a lower octave. "Killing a child's sickly father and kidnapping him, only to dump him with others, who then dumped him again because he failed to grow into a killer they could be proud of!"

She clenched her teeth, resisting the urge to snarl back that he should be thanking her for rescuing him from growing up in a flophouse until his premature death from neglect. "Your father was already on his way out, albeit slowly. I asked him, begged him really, to let me place you in a home where you'd be cared for and nurtured in a way that he couldn't. He said, T'ain't no one gon' take my boy away, not for no reason."

She fixed her gaze on Daniel's face but didn't attempt to exert control this time. She simply told the truth. "Last time I tried, he told me that he didn't even let your bitch mamma — his words — take you, so he certainly wasn't gonna allow some gal from the state t'get away with it."

Danny's mouth sagged open. "He said… my mother wanted to take me? But that's not—"

"What he told you? No, I'm sure not. It was certainly a departure from the original story he gave me." She considered stopping, but the way Danny looked at her and his accusatory tone bothered her. She was surprised at how much. "I did some sniffin' around after that. Literally, I walked 'round that sorry property one night using my full senses, somethin' I hadn't had call to do on previous visits. Know what I found?"

Danny shrank back in the chair, shaking his head. As if he already knew, making her wonder if, on some level, he'd always suspected the truth. "A body. In a shallow grave, in the dirt patch behind your building's parking lot. I dug it up, and sure 'nough, it was a woman's remains with her skull bashed in."

"No." Danny shook his head so hard she worried he might rattle his brains. "No! That's crazy, that... he wasn't like that! He was never violent, never mean —"

"To you, no, I agree. His neglect of you was not due to a lack of affection or wicked nature, like most of my... special cases." She shrugged, palms up. "Maybe I should have stayed silent 'bout this. But it burdens me to think that you've spent all these years believin' me so cruel, so arbitrary, that I would have taken you from a man whose only crimes were poverty and poor health."

"I... I'm going to be..." Danny jumped up and dashed into her bathroom.

She listened to his retching and sighed. Plucking at a loose thread on the plain white quilt covering her legs, she wondered whether she had been too direct. Humans were so delicate, as easy to wound emotionally as they were physically. Once again, she felt grateful for the gift of her stoic and practical nature.

When Danny returned, his complexion was a shade paler than normal. He stood at the foot of the bed, regarding her with bloodshot eyes. "Thank you for telling me."

She cocked her head to one side and blinked. She hadn't expected that. "You... believe me then. Understand why I did what I did?"

He shrugged one shoulder. "I don't see why you'd bother lying. While it might burden you that I thought you just up and killed my father, I don't believe you're capable of caring about my feelings on the subject so much that you'd bother making this up."

He grasped the footboard of her bed with both hands and leaned forward. "While I was barred from any assignments related to you, that hasn't kept me from gaining access to the Wrangler's records. They've come to suspect what you've been up to regarding the occasional parent vanishing. However, they're not law enforcement, so they've taken a liberal stance on... the differing ethical standards of non-humans." His expression told her he didn't necessarily agree with that position. "Anyway, since every single one of your possible victims was a confirmed child abuser of the nastiest sort, and you've managed not to arouse public suspicion, they haven't felt compelled to act."

He raked his fingers through his wavy black hair. "Anyway, the only outlier was the first parent to vanish, my father. Except... he wasn't an outlier, now, was he?" His voice cracked. "He was a god-damned murderer. He killed my mom when she decided to leave him."

Eva nodded. "Yes. Mostly to keep you, I believe. Which was why I was certain he'd never relinquish you, not even to ensure your survival. He might have loved you in his way, but he also considered you property. Your welfare surely was not his priority."

"You could have just told the cops. Led them to my mother's... to her, and let the legal system run its course." He shook his head slowly. "I know I can't expect you to think like a human entirely, but you've lived in our world most of your long life. You can't pretend not to understand how things are supposed to be done."

She marveled at him. Even though he was a grown-ass man, he still retained the naiveté of a child. "What d'you think would've happened if I did that? How would I have explained locating your mamma's body, hm? And even if I'd somehow gotten them to find her based on an anonymous tip, what you think the system would've done to him? To you?"

He crossed his arms tightly and looked out the window for a spell. "They'd have investigated. Maybe would've eventually found evidence my father did it, arrested him, and sent him to prison where he would've died a lingering death alone in the infirmary." His shoulders slumped. "And put me in the foster care system."

She nodded. "But with the added wildcard of whilst they took the time of investigatin', your daddy might just have gotten it into his head to either run off with you — unlikely given his ill health — or quite possibly killed you and himself like I seen so many do thinkin' they'll be reunited in some magical afterlife. All's I did was eliminate the worst possible outcome for your own good — and arguably even his."

Danny scoffed. "Come on, that wasn't your only motivation. None of the kids you've taken... it's really all about extending the existence of your kind, not about selflessly rescuing innocent children."

She considered his accusation. "Fine, you're not all wrong. As I confessed when you was knee-high to a grasshopper, I am not a maternal creature. That's me, though. Others of my kind are, and their longin' for a young'un goes beyond merely continuing our kind. We are dyin' out, boy. Less of us born each generation, to the point where a natural cub is near unheard of anymore. Like any species, we want to go on."

She flashed him a smile. "I could take anyone's kid, you know. The child playing in the backyard down the road, one who wanders off from vacationers who look away for just a moment... anybody's. Fact that I only ever take the ones whose lives would otherwise have ended early and in tears should tell you somethin'."

He tilted his head to the left. "Which is?"

"I am not a monster. Well, least not entirely."

Danny broke the ensuing silence first. "I know that. I've had some hard feelings about you and yours for a long time. Being taken, being rejected... I couldn't figure out why you bothered choosing me in the first place." A sudden, horrifying realization crossed his face. "Wait a minute. Is that why... did you think because my father was a killer that I was destined to grow up the same?"

"That you might have inherited certain personality traits that would contribute to your becomin' a successful predator?" She considered before deciding to remain honest. He could bear it. "It did play into my decision to not just turn you over immediately to a human foster family. Certain genetic predispositions tend to make it easier to accept the darker side of my kind's nature."

"Dear God." Danny pressed the heels of his hands firmly against his eyes. "Ugh, I know I shouldn't judge you by human standards, but..." He dropped his hands and shook himself from head to toe. "Well, you were wrong, as it turned out. I didn't have it in me, and so here I am, still an ordinary human. Sorry to disappoint you."

Eva shrugged. "I am disappointed, but only because I think you would've been happier as one of us. I can sense your anger but also loss and longin'. You wanted to be the cat." She tilted her head back, remembering. "I, too, was adopted into this life, albeit a very long time ago. I cannot imagine havin' experienced the Shift only to lose it forever." She met his gaze again. "I am truly sorry for the pain that has caused you, Danny."

The sudden rush of sympathy and regret for her actions surprised her. It was rare she felt so much and so deeply. She hadn't had this extended or intense an interaction with another in... well, she couldn't recall ever having one. Also, Danny had been her first, the child she had originally thought to make her own. He held a special place in her heart that she hadn't acknowledged until now.

Danny seemed to reach some inner conclusion. "It's in the past. My life… it wasn't always easy, but it led me to where I am now, which means something. I am doing work that is meaningful, on behalf of beings that most people only know about from stories, if at all." He managed a smile. "Maybe I should be thanking you for setting me on the sigogglin trail of switchbacks and dead-ends and narrow escapes that led me to this point in my life. I guess, on some level, I've always known that I owed you. Probably why I chose to save you instead of hauling my Lizard Man back to South Carolina like I'd planned."

Eva couldn't help but smile at his use of Appalachian colloquialism. Apparently, he still retained some memory of his time with her. "Speakin' of, just what are we gonna do about him? As the sayin' goes, he don't have to go home, but he can't stay here."

"No, he sure can't. While it's summertime, the temperature change will have minimal effect, but come winter, the chilly nights won't be good for him." He caught the look she cast his way and rolled his eyes. "Ri-i-i-ight, you only care because he's hunting on your turf." He drew a cellphone from his back pocket and tapped the screen a couple of times. "That tranq I shot him with also contained a micro tracker. And… yep, there he is. Still in the same general area where you came across him."

"That's some fancy tech right there," she noted. "Did you stick one of those in me whilst you was bandagin' me up?"

Daniel hesitated just long enough to make her nervous. "Like I said, you're not my responsibility. If your caseworker wants you tagged, well, that's up to him to do it."

"Caseworker." She chuckled and shook her head. "Well, guess now I know how folks assigned to me feel about that situation. Knowin' someone's keeping track of their activities, might show up whenever and wherever—"

"Why do you look like this now?" Danny sketched a circle in the air in front of his face.

An abrupt changing of the subject, but she went with it. "You mean younger than when we first met."

He nodded. "Yeah, but it's more than that. Your hair, even your features are slightly different unless I'm misremembering."

"It's vampire syndrome."

He blinked. "Excuse me?"

"Vampires in stories have a problem with agin' but not lookin' older. After a while, they have to start changing up their appearance or move away so folks around them don't start askin' questions. Except'in I like where I live. I like this house. You know, when I bought it, it only cost around five grand. Crazy, right?" She tapped the tip of her nose. "Anyhow, after a certain amount of time passes, I 'die' and inherit the house under a new name from my dearly departed auntie or cousin or what-have-you. Violet became Drema became Opal became Lora and now Eva. True, we all kinda favor one another, but hey, that's genetics for you, right?"

"So, the Shift does allow you to do more than take on the animal form. You can alter your human appearance as well." He looked smug, adding under his breath, "Thought so."

She cursed herself silently for having forgotten that she wasn't just talking to any old acquaintance but rather one who could pass along what she revealed to an organization intent on managing her. However nicely they tried to dress it up as protection, control was the Wranglers' goal, and she didn't take kindly to that notion at all.

"Well," she said, "now you know where that Lizard Man is, you best call your friends in and take him on home."

"Not sure that's still an option." He slipped his phone back into the pocket of his jeans. "But what about you? I don't want to leave you here all alone when you can hardly move."

She gritted her teeth, swung her legs over the side of the bed, and stood. She managed not to yelp from multiple shooting pains along her back and side. "I'll be a hundred percent within hours," she said. "And I can certainly manage 'til then. So, thanks for getting me back here, but you can go on now." She nodded toward the door.

"Yeah, all right." He didn't look convinced but gathered up his backpack from the corner of her bedroom. "Eva?"

"Yep?"

"It was…" He stared at the ceiling as if hoping to find his next words written across it. "I'm glad I saw you again."

She smiled. "Me too." Again, she was surprised — she actually meant it.

He started off but halted in the doorway. Without looking back, he said, "The Wranglers don't like what you're doing. They've let it slide for a good long while, but that doesn't mean they will forever. And they won't go to the police any more than you did. So, if you're happy here and want to stay, you better consider cutting it the hell out."

She bowed her head. She didn't like it but knew it was solid advice. "I hear you, darlin', and… I'll consider it."

"Hope you do." With that, he disappeared down her hallway. A moment later, she heard her front door open and shut.

Eva sank back in bed with a groan. It would take her a bit longer to heal than she'd let on, but she needed Danny to leave before he got her to reveal anything else that could come back and bite her. Besides, the sooner he got rid of that damned scaly peckerwood, the happier she'd be.

She contemplated his parting shot. The boy was right—if the Wranglers had eyes on her, then she had to make a change. She could stop solving the hard cases her way, but then she'd probably have to give up her job entirely because she wouldn't be able to bear not freeing the kids in direst need of her intervention. Or she could pull up stakes, leave the only territory she'd ever known, and find a new one. The thought of starting over at her age somewhere brand-new was far from appealing.

Of course, there was a third option, but it would be the most challenging. She could reach out to her network, and they could execute something that had only ever been discussed in theory—a joint hunt. They could pool all their information on the Wranglers, track down their bases throughout the country, and wipe them out.

But even if such a massive undertaking could be arranged and covered up successfully, what would that mean for Danny? She doubted he would simply abandon the Wranglers after they had been the only ones to take him in and give him, as he'd put it, a purpose in life. He surely wouldn't sit by and let her kind execute them… and she could not imagine eliminating him, especially not after this reconnection, however brief it had been. And practically, there simply were not enough of hers to take on his, given the Wranglers' use of advanced technology and who-knew-what other resources in addition to their greater numbers.

Eva growled. This situation was a cage of her own forging, and she knew it. She spent the remainder of the day mentally circling within, searching in vain for a way out.

Chapter Nine

The days following Stan's battle with the great cat were exercises in frustration. He slept and shat and satisfied the urgings of his rumbling gut, but his challenger didn't return. He wondered if she had crawled off and died. The thought infuriated him so much that he decided the only way to relieve it was to kill something else — not for food, but distraction.

Which led Stan to venture out during the day (something he normally avoided) and head toward a riverside location where he had seen Unscaled lounging about previously. Today he wasn't going to use that knowledge to avoid detection. Today he wanted to hear screams and have fun.

Completely unaware that they had chosen the wrong sunny weekend for a camping trip along the Williams River, the vacationing Borden family of Bristol, Rhode Island, were blissfully cleaning up the remains of their breakfast. Well, not entirely blissfully. The father, Andy, was a middle-aged man of middling height with thinning brown hair and steel-framed glasses perched midway between the bridge and tip of his nose. He stood with his arms folded across his fishing vest-wrapped chest, glaring at his mirror-image (though shorter and with much more hair) son, ten-year-old Emery, who had just thrown a strip of bacon at his older sister Eliza's face.

"Ha, you got dead animal on you! Now you're evil like the rest of us," Emery crowed.

"Ewwwww!" Eliza leapt to her feet, narrowly dodging the strip of flying fatty meat. "You disgusting little… carnivore! Keep the remains of your victim to yourself!" She pursed her pink lipstick-coated lips into a moue of contempt. "Pigs are as smart as three-year-old children. Would you eat a three-year-old kid, huh?"

"I dunno." Emery shrugged. "Do they taste like bacon?"

"We were supposed to cast off a half-hour ago," intoned Andy. Clad in his waders, bait box at his feet, and rod in hand, he had been ready to go far longer. "Emery, stop fooling around and move it!" He reluctantly dragged his gaze to meet the familiar annoyance reflected in his daughter's cornflower blue eyes. "You're still welcome to join us, you know."

Eliza planted her fists on her hips and scowled as only a pre-teen judging their parent can. "I told you, I am not going to slaughter poor, innocent fish for sport."

"You mean for yummy food we're going to fry up and eat later?" Emery sneered. He mimed picking up a fish by its tail and swallowing it whole with one hand while rubbing his belly with the other.

"You don't have to go fishing, pumpkin." Abigail Borden stuck her head out of the yurt in which she'd been stowing the breakfast plates. "We can take a nice hike through the woods instead."

Andy forced a smile. "That's right, you go and check out the... plants and trees. I'm sure it'll be lots of fun. Emery, get your waders on and let's go."

Emery scrambled to his feet. "Okay, Dad." He hesitated. "Um, where are my waders?"

Andy sighed wearily. Abigail replied, "Check your suitcase, bud."

"I don't know why you had to drag me on this stupid trip," Eliza muttered as her brother vanished into the yurt to don his gear. "You know I hate this outdoorsy stuff. Nothing but bugs and heat during the day and bats and cold at night." She spread her arms wide. "The woods are meant for animals, not people."

"It's meant for people to enjoy some peace and quiet," Andy said. "I brought you with us so we could spend quality time as a family." Like couples' therapist Dr. Cohen had recommended during his last one-on-one session, but he kept that to himself.

"That's right, dear." Abigail emerged garbed in mom jeans, a designer flannel shirt, and sneakers not at all meant for walking in the woods. She tucked her blonde-highlighted red hair underneath a baseball cap with Tesla stitched across the front. "Time together and away from other distractions is exactly what this family needs." She glanced briefly at her husband. Dr. Cohen had told her this trip was probably their last shot at remaining a family, but she kept that to herself.

"Whatever." Eliza picked up a can of bug spray and stepped away from the group to spray herself from head to toe. She might be trapped in this weekend from hell watching her parents pretend they weren't totally sick of each other, but she didn't have to compound it by going home with Lyme disease or malaria or whatever else lurked in this miserable, seemingly endless forest. She reached overhead and spritzed down her back.

A loud hiss came from directly behind her.

She froze. What if she had sprayed a snake accidentally, and it would suffocate because she, as a human, had no business bumbling through nature spraying poison around? Guilt (and more than a dollop of fear) spurred her to whirl around while exclaiming, "Oh, poor danger noodle. Did I...?" She broke off, confused, as she found herself staring not at a gassed snake but rather at a broad, scale-covered chest.

She looked up, up, up to a neck and head that belonged to something so beyond her ability to assimilate that her mind simply said nope and left her standing there, mouth agape and eyes wide.

Stan looked down at the small Unscaled female and coughed as its noxious scent clung to his mucus membranes. He'd never known an Unscaled could unleash spray like those small, striped furries he'd learned to avoid the hard way in his swamp. The burning sensation in his throat and nasal passages only fueled his aggression. He raised his claws and roared spittle across the face gawping stupidly up at him.

That was enough to free Eliza of her shocked, silent paralysis. She swung around and bolted back toward her family, waving her arms and screaming, "MonstermonstermonsterRUN!"

Andy, who had already stomped off downriver with Emery in tow, spun around at his daughter's shrieking. "What in the hell's gotten into...?"

Emery kept right on walking. "Probably stepped on an ant and is off to kill herself."

Meanwhile, Abigail blinked furiously as she struggled to reconcile known reality with the vision of a seven-foot-tall lizard running on its hind legs after her wailing daughter. Motherly instinct seized control of the situation almost immediately. She ducked back into the yurt and came out holding the small ax Andy used to chop firewood. As Eliza sprinted past her, Abigail raised the ax and swung, clotheslining the lizard creature with the blade.

Stan howled as another Unscaled female appeared and struck him with something hard and sharp across his middle. His scales absorbed most of the impact, but his own momentum had allowed the blade to penetrate deeply enough to cause significant pain. And (as previously established) Stan really hated pain.

Brought up short, the huge lizard monster staggered back from Abigail as its dark blood leaked out from the jagged tear in his midsection. She hefted the ax overhead and shouted, "You want some more? Get away from my daughter, whatever you are, or I'll fucking end you!"

Stan roared back at the noisome Unscaled female and swiped her aside with one thick arm. She went flying into a nearby tangle of bushes with a screech, and her weapon thudded to the ground. Satisfied, Stan turned back to pursue the still-fleeing smaller female.

"Abs!" Andy cried, sprinting back to their campsite. He staggered to a halt in front of what appeared to be a very large man clad in lizard skin and an impressive but certainly rubber mask with virulently red eyes. "Hey, you, whatever game you're playing, get away from my family and go play it somewhere else!" He waggled his forefinger under the perturbingly tall man's chin.

Stan blinked his nictitating membranes. This Unscaled appeared to be offering a piece of himself as food, perhaps to save the others. He took a bite and chewed the sample, evaluating whether the Unscaled's sacrifice was acceptable.

Andy's mouth fell open. The ragged stump where his index finger used to be pulsed blood across the scaly costume of the maniac — for surely that's what he had to be. Then the pain and nausea of in-stantaneous amputation struck him, and he dropped to his knees, clasped his mangled hand to his chest, and yowled.

By now, the ruckus had drawn Emery's attention. Before the monster could eat more of his father, he ran at it, gripping his fishing rod like the knights he'd once seen at Medieval Times held their lances. "Leave my dad alone!" He aimed toward the creature's already wounded belly and jabbed the gash with all his might.

Stan howled as the tip of the small Unscaled's stick pierced his already torn flesh and skated along a rib. He slashed down and broke the stick in two, then yanked out the portion stuck inside himself and flung it away. But before he could do the same to the little Unscaled male, something struck him in the small of his back, although not hard enough to pierce his hide this time. He spun around and saw the first female again, only now she had the second's weapon in her hands.

It had taken all of Eliza's courage to stop racing through the forest away from the lizard creature and double back to check on her family. They might be pains in her ass to varying degrees, but they were still hers, and she wasn't going to abandon them to be killed by some discount Godzilla.

"I swear I will chop you into bite-sized chunks and… barbecue them for dinner if you don't get the hell away from us!" She brandished the ax, planted her feet the way she'd learned in softball, and prepared to swing for the bleachers.

"Whatever you are, you'd better run." Abigail limped over to join her daughter. Her hair, no longer contained by her cap, had been rendered a frizzy, flaming mane threaded with brambles. She grasped her pink lady's multitool with the longest blade extended and jabbed it into the lizard man's thigh.

Emery thrust the jagged edge of his broken fishing pole at the lizard beast's face. "Come at me, bro," he taunted. "I double-dog dare you!"

"Owwwwww," moaned Andy, still a huddled heap of blood loss and shock on the ground.

None of this was going as Stan had planned. He was beyond furious, wounded, and the bit of Unscaled he'd gotten to eat had been wholly unsatisfying. He decided to rip the heads off all these annoying beings and then go have a sulk in the mud. But as he raised his arm, claws cocked and ready to sever, a new voice startled him.

"Back away from the Lizard Man!" Daniel ran out of the woods, tranq gun cocked and held in his right hand while waving away the people surrounding his charge with the left. "Get back, now! I've got him." He came up alongside the bruised, dirtied, and disheveled woman, grasped her shoulder, and pulled her back several feet, then did the same with the girl holding the ax. He jabbed his forefinger at the young boy with the broken rod and then indicated with a jerk of his thumb that he should join the others.

"Fine, but I totally had him," the boy grumbled as he reluctantly obeyed.

Daniel interposed himself between the wounded man on the ground and the Lizard Man. His heart was thudding so hard that he assumed everyone could hear it. When his tracker had indicated the cryptid was on the move in daylight and heading toward a frequently populated area, he'd hightailed it into the state park as fast and as far in as he could by Jeep. Now he stood face-to-face with his charge for the first time, and he felt equally thrilled and terrified.

Daniel swallowed against the dryness spreading rapidly through his mouth and throat. He raised his free hand and spread his fingers wide. "I know you're scared, but I'm not here to hurt you. It's just that you don't belong here, my friend, so I'm going to take you home. Okay?" He raised the tranq gun quickly and took aim at the agitated creature's neck.

Stan recognized the weapon this newly arrived Unscaled held. It was a bark-hurt, and it frightened him far more than anything else the other Unscaleds had threatened him with. So much so that instinct immediately took over, and in virtually the same instant it was pointed at him, he dropped to all fours and launched himself forward, head lowered.

Air exploded out of Daniel's lungs as the Lizard Man headbutted him in the stomach, the tranq gun sliding free of his suddenly nerveless fingers. He landed on his back, gasping for breath with the Lizard Man crouched over him. Glowing red eyes fixed on his, mouth wide open around rows of spiked teeth.

"N... no, p... please," Daniel managed to gasp. "I'm n... not trying to..." But that was as far as he got.

Stan threw his head back and bellowed in triumph. Finally, he had a target for his displeasure completely at his mercy. He raised his claws but realized one swipe would end it, and he wanted to savor this. So instead, he curled his giant hands into fists and began hammering the Unscaled male repeatedly.

Daniel barely had time to wrap his arms around his face and head, shielding them as much as possible before the enraged Lizard Man rained hell down on him. He heard as well as felt his bones crack. Searing pain flooded his senses like he hadn't experienced since he went through the Shift as a boy. This was it. This was how he was going to die.

Meanwhile, Stan felt nothing but relief at making someone else suffer for all his disappointments, all his thwarted desires. For the constant flashing lights and sounds and invasions of his privacy. For the loss of his home and his tasty-softs. For all the Unscaled whose screams hurt his ears and whose weapons hurt his body. For the squawking fowl he'd missed out on tasting and for these pesky Unscaleds he'd hoped to have fun with but instead had the audacity to fight back. For the one actual challenge he'd hoped to encounter again but couldn't seem to find—the soft yet pointy cat with eyes bright as the stars that used to shine down on his swamp at night.

Something hit Stan between his neck and left shoulder, biting deeply enough to cut muscle and bone, rendering his arm instantly useless. Bellowing in agony, he swiveled his head around and saw the other male Unscaled standing there, sharp-edged weapon dripping liquid Stan knew belonged inside him. The male raised the weapon again and yelled, a clear threat to continue chopping Stan into pieces.

Not wanting that at all, Stan stood, hissed at each of the still-standing Unscaled in turn, and ran back into the depths of the forest.

Andy watched as the giant bastard who'd attacked them sprinted away. He dropped the ax and bent over nearly double, wheezing as his last drop of adrenaline dribbled away. His gaze fell across the park ranger or whoever he was lying motionless on the ground. "Is that guy okay?"

Abigail and Eliza knelt on either side of the wounded man. Meanwhile, Emery remained slightly away from the huddle facing the woods, broken fishing rod clenched in both fists, standing guard against the monster's return.

Abigail tapped the motionless man's shoulder gingerly. "Sir? Can you hear me?"

"Are you kidding, Mom?" Eliza bit her trembling lower lip and swiped at the tears streaking mascara down her cheeks. "Look at him!"

Andy dropped to his knees, not entirely by choice. He quickly stripped off his vest and shirt. He wrapped the latter around his hand to slow the bleeding from the stump of his forefinger, then turned his attention to the injured man. Eliza was right—to say the guy was in rough shape was an understatement. Although he'd wisely attempted to shield his head from being bashed in, the creature had gotten through his guard more than a few times. One of his arms was clearly broken, and blood flowed from his nose, ears, and split lips. "Geeze, that psycho really beat him into the dirt."

Abigail pressed her fingertips against the side of the man's neck. "He's got a pulse." She offered her husband a smile. "That's good. Right?" Her jaw began to tremble, and tears welled up in her eyes.

Andy scooted over and draped his left arm around her shoulders. "Yeah, that's really good, love." He nuzzled her hair as the reality of how close they'd all come to being in the same or worse shape as their battered hero hit home. "Abs, you were amazing protecting our girl. Thank God you're all right."

She reached for his wrapped hand and hesitated. "If you hadn't driven that thing off, I don't know... oh, my God, Andy, your finger!" She began scanning the ground frantically. "If we can find it and get it in the cooler, maybe —"

He shook his head. "It's gone. That... whoever, whatever he was, ate it." He swallowed against a fresh wave of nausea

"Oh. Oh, my God." Abigail repeated the words as she sobbed against his shoulder.

"It's okay, Mom. Dad." Eliza held up her cell phone and waggled it. "I managed to get a signal and called 9-1-1. They're coming, and maybe they can, you know, do something for him." She looked down at the unconscious man and winced. "Is it wrong that I'm glad this isn't one of you?" She looked from her mother to her father and bit her lower lip to stop it from trembling.

Her parents spread their arms and gathered her in a tight hug.

Emery glanced at them, then toward the woods, then back at his family. He doubted the lizard monster would return, not after they'd taught him not to mess with the Bordens. So, he dropped his fishing pole, rejoined his family, and stretched his arms as wide as possible to wrap his parents and sister in a protective embrace.

CHAPTER TEN

"Suppose now I understand why Willa and her mate rejected him," muttered the elderly woman standing in the threshold. "Boy might just be too stupid to live."

"Ma'am?" The duty nurse, Tammy, looked up from the chart in which she'd been making notes. This visitor, a slightly stooped woman with silver-white hair twisted into a bun, wasn't the first or even the second to stop by since Mr. Smith's release from ICU earlier in the week, although the others had come in groups. First was the grateful family he had come to the aid of when he was viciously attacked by either a rabid animal or serial killer or some Black Lagoon-esque creature (the news reports varied, and Tammy wasn't sure which story to believe). The second had identified themselves only as work colleagues. Mr. Smith is one popular fellow, Tammy thought. Pity he's too comatose to enjoy their visits.

"Don't mind me, sweetie. Just thinking out loud." The old woman crossed the room to Mr. Smith's bedside. Tammy noticed how smoothly she moved for someone of her advanced years. "How's he doing?"

"Are you family, ma'am?" Tammy asked.

"Sure am. His auntie." Her brief smile revealed long, yellowish teeth.

Oddly, Tammy found herself remembering a children's book illustration of the wolf dressed as Red Riding Hood's grandmother and suppressed a shiver. "Mr. Smith's condition is stable, but he isn't out of the woods yet. He suffered serious internal injuries and multiple bone fractures. The concussion—"

The elderly woman's pale gold eyes bore into hers. "You all finished in here now, right? Got other patients to see."

Tammy realized she was all finished for now and had other patients to see. She tucked the chart back into its pocket at the foot of Mr. Smith's bed. "Now, don't you stay too long, ma'am. It'll be dark soon. Have a nice visit."

Eva waited until she heard the nurse's footsteps heading down the hallway before she went over to the door and pulled it closed. Then she returned to Danny's side. "My apologies for being snide earlier. I just don't understand why you went after your overgrown lizard all alone." She studied him with a frown. "Now look at you, all rode hard and put away wet."

She had expected to receive some sort of message once Danny had tracked the Lizard Man down, telling her to lie low because he'd called in other Wranglers to help haul the invader out of her territory. When days passed with no contact whatsoever, she'd become curious and then concerned. She'd checked the local news online and found an article about a family that had been attacked by a madman in a lizard suit, then realized the heroic but critically injured fellow who'd saved them had to be Danny. As there was only one hospital in the vicinity, it had been simple enough for her to find him, but then she'd spied a team of Wranglers lurking around and been forced to Shift her appearance before visiting.

She shook her head. "Quite the gom you got us both in. Wranglers showed up, after all, if'n a bit too late to do you any good. Guess 'cause you didn't check in, or they caught the news coverage. Either way, here am I havin' to walk around lookin' like my own great-granny to sneak on in here." She gently brushed a stray dark curl away from Danny's bruised temple. "Not that you're lookin' right peart your own self."

He remained silent and still, covered in bandages and bruises and tubes and wires. Eva gnawed her lower lip, troubled by emotions familiar and foreign. She knew the other Wranglers showing up meant she should already be packed and running as fast and far away as possible. Yet she couldn't bear the thought of that thrice-damned intruder into her territory getting away with what he'd done to her boy.

It hurt her heart to even consider leaving him in this helpless, hopeless condition. Everything in the nurse's demeanor told her that Danny wasn't expected to recover, and her own senses confirmed that grim prognosis.

"I don't think these fine medical professionals can help you. But just maybe I can." She argued back at herself, "Except if'n I do, and the others find out, they might come and shred me for supper. Then again, they don't have to find out, do they? I mean, you'll keep it quiet for your own sake if not mine... although there's your loyalty to them Wranglers—"

She shook her fists at the ceiling. "Consarn it, you senile old biddy! You can stand around debatin' your own self all night, or you can do what you damn well know you came here intendin' to!"

Decided, she stooped over Daniel and whispered into his ear, "I didn't do right by you, darlin'. I meant well, but I didn't follow through, and your sufferin' growing up is on me. Now, I can't change none of that, but this time, I'm gonna follow through. 'Cause lyin' here locked in your own noggin until you wither away ain't no kind of future, least none I can abide for you." She closed her eyes briefly. "I only hope you come to see that what I'm about to do, I'm doin' for your own good."

She traced the path of the tube inserted into the back of his left hand to the bag of blood hanging from a hook on a steel pole beside his bed. Eva studied the valve between the tube and the bag. "It is a shame you never got to experience the ritual of becoming one of us." She removed the partially empty bag from the hook and disconnected the tube. "It's an incredible experience learnin' how to Shift, and the first time you accomplish it your own self?" She opened the valve at the bottom of the bag and squeezed the remaining blood into her mouth. "Mm, O negative. The electricity in the air, the blood sharin', the shed of your singular self to embrace duality—nothin' else compares."

She extended the fingernail of her right forefinger into a claw and made a short lengthwise slice along her left wrist. She pressed the slit in her vein firmly against the open valve on the blood bag and squeezed her fist. "Unfortunately, there's no time for formal rituals and suchlike now. And, I must tell you, I'm not entirely sure this'll even accomplish anything. I mean, it should because Shift magic is blood magic, and it flows through these here veins. But without the chants and other formalities?" She shrugged. It was a roll of the bones, no doubt, but a gamble well worth taking given the grim alternative.

Once the bag was nearly full, she reattached the tubing and hung it back up on the hook. She watched for several seconds to confirm it was dripping her blood rapidly and steadily into Danny's veins. Satisfied, she swiped her palms against one another twice. "Well, that's it then. Here's hopin'."

She licked her wrist until the flesh knit itself back together, pulse throbbing loudly in her ears. What she was doing went far beyond what her kind would consider acceptable—particularly given that Danny had been rejected previously, not to mention he was a Wrangler and thus a significant potential threat.

Then again, her people's fierce individuality meant they had no formal laws or self-policing. Sure, some might be angry. One or more might even decide to challenge her for defiling the sanctity of the Shift and potentially exposing their kind. But that was all they could do.

Danny groaned softly. His left fingers twitched.

Eva smiled as a tremendous weight she'd barely acknowledged fell away. "Fuck it. Let 'em come." She ran her tongue over her lips and lapped up stray droplets of blood.

She leaned over and kissed Danny lightly on his cheek. "Sleep tight, boy. Time for me to go home and rest my own self." She strode to the door with confidence and energy that belied her illusion of frailty. "Oh, and don't you worry none 'bout that damned lizard what done this to you. I shall be solvin' that particular problem come nightfall."

CHAPTER ELEVEN

"Amazing!" Lester Samuels, the Wrangler in charge of Eva, scratched the top of his balding head. "Last time we saw you, man, the doctors were telling us all the reasons not to hold out hope you'd open your eyes again. Yet here you are."

"Here I am." Daniel stared into the middle distance, barely paying attention to the visiting pair of Wranglers. He was too busy struggling to process his feelings, physical and otherwise, since awakening that morning.

Chief Alannah Moore, still as physically imposing a woman in her mid-fifties as when he'd met her more than a decade ago, was studying him like a microbe in a petri dish. "Not that we're unhappy at your sudden rally, Smith, but it defies expectations."

He glanced up and read suspicion etched in every line on her face. "Don't know what you want me to tell you, Chief. All I remember is the Lizard Man on me, beating me… then pain and the certainty…." His throat muscles tightened, leaving him only able to think the rest: I was about to die.

So how was he alive?

Chief Moore huffed an audible breath. "You should never have gone after the Lizard Man on your own." Daniel opened his mouth to explain again, but she raised her hand in a silencing gesture. "I realize there were people in imminent danger, and you were the only Wrangler on site. My point is that as soon as you had narrowed his location to the Monongahela, you should have called in reinforcements immediately, before the attack occurred."

Daniel bit back an insubordinate retort. She was right. He also knew he couldn't admit the real reason he hadn't summoned backup. He'd feared that if he summoned a team, they would have put the Lizard

Man down. The cryptid had strayed too far from his domain and left too much mayhem in his wake. While Daniel understood the logic of eliminating him from a public-safety perspective, the idea of it hurt his very soul.

If he admitted as much to Chief Moore, though, she would chalk it up to evidence of his overly emotional attachment to the subject and likely reassign him to permanent desk duty or dismiss him altogether. So instead, he said, "You're right, Chief. I screwed up. Thought I could contain him myself, but he's not following his previous patterns of behavior."

"No, he is not. He's gone from hiding and avoiding humans to committing overtly hostile acts." She fixed her steely gaze on him. "Did you at least manage to tag him?"

He hadn't told them about his first encounter with the Lizard Man to keep Eva out of it, only that he'd tracked the creature to somewhere in the Monongahela. Impulsively, he lied, "No, I'm afraid not. I haven't been able to get close to him until… and then I didn't get off a shot before he tackled me."

"Unfortunate," the chief grumbled. "Regardless, we came in a Mobile Field Office, so we have all the equipment necessary to locate him. Park's huge, but we've been able to narrow down where he might have gone to ground after the attack." She shook her head slowly. "Good thing the father was so easy to convince it was just some loon in a costume, and the mother's still too deep in shock to make a convincing argument otherwise. As for the kids, well, everyone's just chalking up their version up to imaginations run wild."

"Chief, what are you planning to do if you find him?" Daniel needed to hear her say it.

She deliberately avoided his gaze and spoke as though reciting pre-rehearsed lines. "After careful review and consideration of numerous civilian reports of Lizard Man attacks, we've determined his violence has escalated beyond our reasonable ability to contain. As a result, he will be removed. Tonight."

Daniel knew she didn't mean simply dragged back to Scape Ore. Despite their terrifying and near-fatal encounter, a wave of grief washed over him. He had failed to contain his charge, and now this incredible being was going to be exterminated.

Anger flared. What right did they have? If it weren't for the decades of encroachment by humans on his swamp, the Lizard Man would probably still be lurking there quietly, seemingly as eternal as he was unique. The Wranglers could have focused on safeguarding his territory in at least a dozen different ways. Instead, they'd chosen to remain uninvolved, save for placing occasional strategic, contemptuous rebuttals of Lizard Man sightings in the media.

"Uhhh, Dan?" Lester said.

He blinked free of his dark thoughts and met Lester's wide-eyed stare. "What?"

"It's just, you're kind of... growling, man."

Daniel stiffened. He turned his attention to the roiling sensation deep in his chest and realized, yes, indeed, he seemed to be making a rumbling sound. He pressed his sternum and breathed deeply until it stopped. "Sorry. I... don't know what that... I'm not feeling myself." A lame response, but honest.

"Your recovery thus far could almost be considered miraculous." Chief Moore side-eyed Lester. "Makes you wonder, doesn't it?"

Lester cleared his throat and stared at his shoes.

Daniel shrugged. "I can't begin to tell you what I don't know myself." Which was also true, although he had a growing suspicion he chose not to share.

Since regaining consciousness, he'd been experiencing periodic bursts of energy during which he could swear he felt his insides shifting, bones and organs mending. His head had felt like it was ablaze, yet he'd sensed it was a healing fire. Meanwhile, doctors kept showing up and shaking their heads in wonderment, poking and prodding and inquiring about his every function and sensation. It was obvious they had not expected him to survive and couldn't point to any medical treatment as the source of his recovery.

Which left Daniel with less scientific possibilities to consider, and from there, only one being who might have provided an... alternate treatment, although he couldn't for the life of him imagine how she'd pulled it off. He also wondered where the hell she was, as he hadn't seen or heard from her yet. His only clue that she had been there came from one of his nurses, who'd commented on how nice it was that his 'sweet old auntie' had popped by.

Chief Moore regarded him for more uncomfortable moments. "We need to meet up with the rest of the team," she said finally. "Take it easy, Smith." She tapped Lester's shoulder and jerked her head toward the door.

"Yeah, man, really glad you're doing better." Lester smiled broadly. "Don't you worry about Mr. Lizard. He won't be hurting anyone else."

Daniel nodded, unable to feign a positive response. He watched as they headed off to the execution, heart sinking like a boulder through quicksand.

Abruptly, his entire body shuddered as though an icicle had been driven through his spinal cord. He gripped the rails along either side of his bed, resisting the urge to spring out of it. "Goddamn it, Eva," he said through chattering teeth. "What did you do to me?"

His grasp tightened, and the metal groaned in protest. His heart pounded like he was in the middle of a marathon. His senses sharpened until he could make out the spectrum within every beam of fading light coming through his hospital room's single window. He heard machines humming and beeping from rooms down the hall, and beneath those sounds came the drumming of what he soon realized were dozens of human heartbeats.

"I remember feeling this!" He looked down at his body, more than half expecting to see fur sprout. But there was no way he could have been inducted to the Shift in his condition. Besides, a wampus could only extend their power to change a child, and then only temporarily. "Eva couldn't have fully inducted me, not without all the rigamarole... so how is any of this happening?"

Searing hunger swept through him, stronger than he'd ever experienced, along with a desire for dominance. He clenched his teeth against it and shook his head hard. No, he was a human being, and damn it, he would remain one!

Daniel forced himself to inhale slowly and deeply. A myriad of scents filled his nasal passages — medicinal, cleansing, shit, and yes, blood. The latter brought a surge of excitement and longing that terrified him.

"Breathe, just breathe!" He screwed his eyes shut and concentrated on his own pulse thrumming in his ears, willing it to slow down. He had no idea how much time had passed, but finally, he began to relax. His hands slipped off the bedrails. When he opened his eyes, he saw dents where his fingers had been.

Sagging against the elevated bed, he realized that his headache was entirely gone, and his body barely registered any discomfort. He felt certain that, within the cast on his right arm, his broken tibia was fully healed. His gaze wandered to the I.V. in his left hand. The power is in the blood, his foster mother once said. Could Eva have somehow transfused her blood into him? That was the only explanation; her healing factor was accelerating his recovery.

"Think your cure comes with side effects, lady cat." He glanced at the crumpled bedrails. "Significant ones."

Meanwhile, where was Eva? If she cared enough to take such drastic action to save his life, why hadn't she bothered to find out whether it worked? Maybe she was dodging the Wranglers... except he now knew that she could simply alter her human appearance so they wouldn't recognize her.

Realization punched Daniel in the gut. "Oh, Eva, no. You're going after the Lizard Man, aren't you?"

At least the Wranglers would give him a quick death. Eva would disembowel him unless the Lizard Man prevailed. Considering their previous encounter, she might be the one in grave danger.

Daniel considered his options. Then he pulled out his I.V.

He vaulted off the bed in one fluid motion and landed without so much as a wobble. He located a fresh set of clothes either Eva or one of his fellow Wranglers had kindly hung in the closet and pulled them on. His cellphone was in a baggie, along with his keys and other personal items. Although the screen had been badly cracked in the attack, his phone still turned on and even had a decent amount of juice. He checked his tracking app and, to his relief, found it was still active, revealing the exact location of the Lizard Man deep within the state park.

He glanced at the door, which the chief and Lester had thankfully shut behind them. Still, if he went out that way, he'd no doubt be accosted by hospital staff. Even if he insisted on discharging himself against medical advice, the long wait and signing of forms would be too much of a delay. Hell, it might already be too late.

Daniel looked around until his gaze fell on the window. "Goddamn it."

Heart pounding, he opened the window as wide as it would go, crawled awkwardly across the sill, and onto the small ledge outside. He was facing the back of the hospital, which was good. He was also four stories up, which was... less good.

He curled into a crouch. "You can do this. I mean, normally, you'd probably break both legs... but you're not normal anymore, are you?" Sending up a prayer to whatever deity might be paying attention, he jumped.

CHAPTER TWELVE

Chief Moore drove the Mobile Field Office deep into the Monongahela State Park. It hadn't been as simple to locate the target without a tracker, but at least they knew where to begin — the clearing where the Borden family had been accosted.

Six of the eight-member team fanned out from the family's abandoned campsite in pairs. Moore and Lester remained behind to oversee the operation.

Lester tapped a console set along one side of the huge vehicle. "I might have a hit, Chief."

"You think, or you know?" Moore looked over from her small desk at the back of the MFO.

Lester pushed his wire-rimmed reading glasses up his nose, fiddled with the controls, then nodded. "It's got to be him. Heat signature registers as significantly larger than human and cold-blooded."

"Coordinates?" He read them off, and she grumbled, "Damn, that's rough terrain without trails and no way for us to drive in." Moore entered the coordinates into her laptop and matched them to the deployed units' current locations. "Looks like Jefferson and Goldman are closest — about a mile out." She picked up her walkie. "All units, rendezvous with Goldman and Jefferson. Roundup Formation Gamma. Confirm, over."

Each unit affirmed. "Over and out," Moore said. So far, all was textbook. But she had far too much experience in the field for overconfidence. Cryptids were naturally full of surprises.

"The civilian said he did some damage with an ax." Lester shrugged. "If the target bled out already, this might turn out to be more of a tidy-up."

Moore shook her head. "Unlikely. According to Smith and his predecessors' logs, the Lizard Man has a rapid healing factor."

"Gotcha, Chief." Lester glanced at the sensor. He took off his glasses, rubbed the lenses with his shirttail, and popped them back. "Ma'am? You got the park service to shut down—no overnight campers, no park rangers, right?"

Moore frowned. "Yes, total lockdown, under Cover 19." As far as the park commission knew, her team had been deployed to investigate and remove the "potentially diseased bear" that had attacked the Bordens. "Why?"

"Someone else's out there. Warm-blooded. Except—" He tapped the side of the sensor. "Whoa!"

"Use your words, Samuels." Moore crossed to his side. Peering into the screen revealed red-orange pulses that seemed to flash into view and then vanish, only to reappear a significant distance closer to where her teams were set to converge. "What is that?"

Lester shook his head slowly. "No idea."

"Speculate," Moore snapped.

"I… think they're human. But moving faster than any human can."

Moore scowled and tapped the screen. "Any chance this thing is on the fritz?"

"Unlikely, Chief."

"It's practically caught up to Evans and DeSoto!" She glared at Lester as though it was his fault.

He shrugged. "I suppose it could be an animal—"

"Shit." Moore smacked her forehead. "I knew it. I knew he must've made contact. She must have infected him somehow… he's probably one now too. Goddamn it!" She pounded her fist several times against the opposite steel wall.

Shaken by her outburst, Lester reluctantly asked, "Who… what are you talking about?"

"Smith!" She whirled to face him. "The man was comatose, brain swollen, nearly every organ damaged, with multiple fractures. Hell, half the reason I brought so many of you on this run was to give you the opportunity to say goodbye to a fallen colleague." She pressed her fingertips against her temples. "And then, like magic, he recovers. How is that possible, I ask you? How?"

She plowed on before Lester concocted a response. "I'll tell you how. Not medicine, not science. It was your cat wampus! The one he vowed not to have any relationship with or loyalty to when he joined the Wranglers." She narrowed her eyes. "The one you regularly update him about even though she isn't his assignment."

Lester blustered, but she thrust her hand out. "Don't even. I've known since I took charge of the East Coast five years ago. I let it slide, figuring it was normal for him to be curious, given their history. But this right here?" She jabbed her forefinger at the fast-moving bogey on the screen. "Proves it's more than that."

"I... don't understand," Lester ventured. "What do you think Eva Cather has to do with the Lizard Man or that other bogey?"

She groaned. "Don't you get it? That's Smith out there! Your wampus and Smith's... damn if I know what she is to him, but she's why he's not only alive but about to disrupt our whole operation. I'd bet my pension on it."

Lester peered over his glasses intently. "Are you saying she turned Smith into a catawampus? Because I'm pretty sure she can't just up and do that. Their kind has this whole ritual and —"

Moore's glare made him feel like a simpleton. "She must have figured out a way, and now he's here to pay it forward by rescuing the target."

"But that's crazy." Lester blanched as her face flushed scarlet. "What I mean is, that's not a mountain lion or any sort of giant cat. The cat wampuses can walk upright, sure, and some even have a third set of legs, but they don't run that way. If that is Smith, well, I'm certain he's still mostly a guy."

She shook her head. "Maybe he is mostly 'guy,' but whatever else he's become, he can't be allowed to interfere with our operation."

Lester considered his next words carefully. "With respect, I've known Dan longer than you, and I can say without a doubt that he's a true believer in our primary mission — protecting cryptids."

"Not at the cost of innocent human lives, it ain't." Moore pursed her lips. "The Lizard Man's wanton recklessness shines a spotlight on all our charges, which is in direct contradiction of our mission." She shook her head. "Regardless of the nobility of his motives, Smith has to be stopped."

She snatched up her walkie again. "All units. Be on the look-out for someone human in appearance. Possibly, it is Daniel Smith. If so, he is not a friendly, repeat, not a friendly. Subdue and return to base after the primary assignment is completed. Out."

Lester returned his attention to the long-range heat sensor. He jerked upright. "Ohhhh, shit. We got another bogey."

Moore sucked in a breath so deep her shoulders rose to her ears. "What is this one, Samuels?"

"Unknown, but it's closing on the Lizard Man's suspected location. Large, warm-blooded, and appears to be moving faster than the first... but on all fours."

Raising the walkie again, Moore said, "Make that two unfriendlies, one already close to the primary target. Probable second cryptid... a cat wampus. Catch her if you can." Moore's expression hardened. "Remove her if you must. Over and out."

CHAPTER THIRTEEN

Stan hurt. Again.

It was worse this time — an agony like he'd never experienced before, plus his left arm still wouldn't do anything he wanted it to. His mangled shoulder had taken hours to stop bleeding, and he was still quite woozy. No matter how often he licked the deep wound or how much mud he rolled in, it kept right on gaping and hurting. In fact, it seemed to be spreading wider, as though an invisible force sought to tear his arm completely out of its socket.

He had run as deeply into the woods as he was able following his botched game, until exhaustion forced him to take refuge for the night. He'd spent the next day dragging himself farther along until it occurred to him that there wasn't any point in continuing. He'd then located a mound of mud and woodsy detritus surrounded by a dense copse and flopped onto it.

The night found Stan still lying there, curled into a ball of woe. No desire could penetrate his funk, not even hunger or thirst. He lay in a dreamlike state while his usually poor memory fired off a series of images much clearer than normal. He hissed and groaned as he relived the departure from his beloved swamp, each encounter with an Unscaled and their increasingly painful retaliations along the way to this new home, the brief but thrilling battle with the big soft-but-also-sharp cat beast and ending with his latest grossly misconceived notion to fight an Unscaled family for fun. All of it had led him to this — suffering and wholly unsatisfied.

Oh sure, he had gotten some payback. He was fairly certain he'd successfully ended the intruder by the river who'd meant to bark-hurt him to death. But at what cost? More to the point, to what gain? He had indulged his darkest instincts, and it had gotten him nothing. No food in his belly, no contentment in his heart—just a half-severed arm and a whole lot of regrets.

The man portion of his brain offered just enough self-awareness for Stan to finally acknowledge that the source of his ongoing miseries might be himself. And maybe it was time to just... stop.

A faint growl drew the brooding Stan's attention. He blinked open his primary eyelids and found himself gazing at the great cat as she entered the clearing.

He hoisted his weary carcass into a half-seated position, startled and enthralled, as she slunk majestically through the trees and regarded him with sun-bright eyes. An emotion that was very nearly joy flooded through Stan. Maybe it wasn't quite time to stop after all.

Finally, something was going Stan's way. This would be far better than slowly fading away while besieged by regrets. He would fight, and this time his opponent would be worthy, unlike all those Unscaled who required sharp objects and bark-hurts to best him. As a gesture of appreciation, he hauled himself onto his feet, raised his still-functioning arm, and swiped his claws through the air with a hiss of challenge.

The giant cat launched herself at the Lizard Man, claws extended.

With a roar of pure glee that echoed through the forest, Stan charged to meet her.

CHAPTER FOURTEEN

His run was incredible. Despite the dire circumstances, a part of Daniel wished it didn't have to end.

His speed and stamina were beyond incredible, not to mention the ease with which he ducked branches and circumnavigated obstacles while plunging steadily through the dense woodlands. There weren't any trails in this section of the Monongahela — it was as wild and fierce as he felt, a no-man's land of thick, untamed growth. Yet he was able to maneuver through it like he was born to it.

Like an animal.

Except he wasn't. Not once did he feel the urge to drop to all fours or experience the blazing sensations that signaled the Shift. All he felt was powerful and confident in his instincts. He seemed as human as ever, but his senses, strength, and speed had been jacked up to eleven.

He picked up such strong scents from the hunters and their prey that after a certain point, he didn't need his tracking app anymore. He soon closed in on the closest pair of Wranglers, which meant he had to formulate a plan quickly. How was he going to stop them without inflicting any lasting harm? They were still his teammates, plus they were just following orders. Although... wasn't that the most famous worst excuse for murder?

He also had to intercept Eva at some point and convince her to work with him to capture the Lizard Man rather than slaughter him outright. He had to trust that his words and whatever obligation she apparently felt toward him would be enough to sway her. But that was a bridge to be crossed later.

At least he had a plan. On entering the woods, he smashed the plaster cast on his right arm against a tree until it fell off. Then he'd made a quick stop at his Jeep (which was still where he'd left it before his near-deadly encounter with the Lizard Man) and collected a few items.

Daniel planned to sedate the Lizard Man using his backup tranq gun, which was now tucked into his belt holster along with his remaining tranquilizer cartridges. Once the creature was down, and ideally, with Eva's assistance, he'd haul the Lizard Man back to the Jeep and toss him in the cage for transport to Florida, where Daniel would let him loose deep in the Everglades. It was the only accessible environment suitable to the Lizard Man's needs since a return to Scape Ore was no longer an option. There were still too many tourists on the lookout for him, and of course, the Wranglers would quickly figure out he'd returned and terminate him there.

Florida offered another advantage no other state could provide. Besides having the requisite swamps and climate most suited to the Lizard Man's needs, the state didn't require — or welcome — outside interference with their myriad cryptids. Unfortunately, this would also make it challenging for Daniel to slip in and deposit a new cryptid. Still, he had a contact at Ochopee — Brock, his predecessor as the Lizard Man's guardian, who had retired from the Wranglers and moved to a small community just outside Fort Lauderdale. Although Daniel had only kept in touch with Brock sporadically, he was confident he could convince his predecessor to offer his former charge asylum.

Nearby crackling sounds brought Daniel up short. He closed his eyes and focused on the noises until he determined that, judging by the heaviness of their footfalls, they came from two men. They were walking at a fast clip, and it would take him about fifteen minutes to catch up, moving at a normal pace.

Daniel pulled out his tranq gun and switched the current pair of heavy-dose cartridges with his only two low-doses. He frowned at the weapon before holstering it again, realizing that if he went with this option, Moore would know that he was behind the disruption of her operation. But his unwillingness to harm anyone outweighed his increasingly vain hope of rescuing the Lizard Man anonymously. Whatever consequences he faced after tonight, he would accept.

Daniel sprinted until he caught up to the pair. Slipping behind a thick-trunked tree, he watched as one, Anthony DeSoto, pushed up a low-hanging branch to let his partner, Bill Evans, slip through. "This is worse than when I had to go after my Jersey Devil through the friggin' Pine Barrens during a heat wave," DeSoto grumbled.

"Heh, that's nothing." Evans negotiated his way under one branch while climbing over another blocking his way forward. "This one time, my 'squatch went into heat—"

Daniel drew a breath, aimed, and fired.

DeSoto released the branch abruptly and slapped his shoulder, eyes widening in confusion at the sight of a tranquilizer dart sticking out of it. Then his eyes rolled back in his head, and he slumped to the forest floor.

The branch he'd been holding up snapped down across Evan's back, causing him to trip over the low branch and fall forward in a tangle of limbs both human and tree. "The hell?" Evans glared upward but didn't see his buddy. Then his gaze drifted down. "Ant? What's wrong with—"

That was as far as he got. Daniel fired again, and a dart lodged itself in the center of Evan's chest. A moment later, he was snoring.

Daniel came out from behind the tree and went to each fallen Wrangler's side to confirm they were still breathing. Then he collected his spent cartridges and shoved them into his pocket while taking a moment to appreciate how easy it had been to pinpoint where he should aim and the precision of his results. Gathering the empties was probably a futile gesture, but best not to blatantly advertise that a Wrangler was taking out the field team.

He raised his head and sniffed the air until he caught the scent of two more humans less than a half-mile away and heading east. Then, farther north, the fainter whiff of two more.

Six deployed then. Chief Moore and Lester Samuels must be in the MFO overseeing operations, which made sense given Lester was the second-most senior Wrangler in the field and an expert in remote tracking systems. They had likely already identified the Lizard Man's current position given his cold-blooded physiology, plus the teams seemed to be converging on the target.

He wondered whether their long-range sensors had picked up his presence yet, or Eva's, for that matter. Despite the relatively cool night air, a fresh trickle of sweat rolled down Daniel's spine. No point dwelling on maybes; he had enough certainties to deal with first. Hopefully, they would all go as smoothly as this first strike—but he very much doubted it.

CHAPTER FIFTEEN

Eva's teeth had finally penetrated the scaly hide of the Lizard Man's left thigh when his ham-sized right fist crashed down on the center of her back, driving her to the ground. She recovered quickly, rolling aside before he could follow up with a second blow. Rising to her hind legs, she pounced at the left side of his neck. He was vulnerable there due to his useless left arm, and she meant to take full advantage.

Stan repelled his assailant by dodging and swinging his tail into the knees of her hind legs, knocking her off-balance. Her jaws snapped shut around empty air.

Stan was covered in gouges and bites, and he was delighted. His challenger was indeed proving worthy, and the thrill of battle made him forget his previous moribund thoughts. Even with only one functioning arm, he'd managed to do some visible damage. The cat's fur was matted in a few places with her blood and his. He wasn't holding anything back because he didn't have to. This kill would be far from easy, but once accomplished, truly earned.

Eva, who had dropped back to all fours and was pacing rapidly while planning her next strike, abruptly stopped in her tracks. The Lizard Man had stretched his maw wide to reveal a riot of fangs that gleamed in the moonlight. Was he... smiling? Her dominant instincts flared at his audacity. She had already been forced to acknowledge that this would be no easy victory. Wounded or not, the enormous creature was so far matching her nearly blow for blow. A growl of irritation rumbled through her chest. It seemed she was going to have to elevate her game.

Stan raised his right claw in preparation to slice down the length of her spine, but then the cat did something so unexpected it stopped him cold. She made odd noises, then rose slowly upright and extruded two more limbs from her upper waist. He flicked his nictitating membranes across his eyes in wonderment. Their battle no longer felt fair, given he only had three functioning limbs, and she now had six. Then again, he had wanted a challenge.

Eva took full advantage of the Lizard Man's obvious confusion after witnessing her full self-manifestation. She dropped back to all six feet and sprang. The impact toppled him backward as she dug her claws into his thighs, ribs, and upper chest and rode him down with a triumphant roar.

Chapter Sixteen

Daniel spied Jimmy Yeoh and Amos Detwiler, noting they had their weapons drawn and maintained a defensive two-person formation as they proceeded, covering one another's backs. Well, that answered one question—Moore had, at minimum, figured out that someone else was disrupting her operation, and she had notified the still-standing teams. Unfortunately, he was out of low-dose tranqs, and the next higher dosage would almost definitely stop a human's heart. Cursing softly, he moved ahead with his alternate plan to minimize damage while still achieving his objective.

Detwiler, a middle-sized but heavily muscled young man, pivoted to confront the sudden noise behind him. "Show yourself!"

"Don't shoot! I am, it's just... I'm not moving so good right now." Daniel struggled to push through the thick tangle of branches leading into the small clearing where Detwiler and Yeoh stood. He clutched his middle, face contorted with pain. "Damn ribs are killing me."

"Smith, what in the hell you doin' out here?" Detwiler kept his tranq gun trained on him.

Yeoh tilted his head to one side as Daniel stumbled into the clearing and raised his hands to shoulder height, wincing. "You should still be in the hospital," he said.

"Yeah, I should," Daniel agreed with a wry smile. "Which should tell you how important this is to me that I've come out here against all medical advice."

"Chief said to keep an eye out for you, boyo." Detwiler grinned but without a trace of humor. "You mean to get in our way? 'Cause that won't turn out like you hope."

Daniel shook his head. "Not like you're thinking, Amos. I mean, clearly, how could I get in your way, even if I was in tip-top shape?" He chuckled as though the very thought were ludicrous. "No, I'm just here to try and convince you — with words — to do the right thing and not execute the Lizard Man tonight."

Yeoh regarded Daniel silently as he limped a bit closer. "You can use your words over there," he said with a hint of warning. "Our hearing is excellent."

Daniel stopped obediently. "Please, just hear me out. I know the Lizard Man's caused some trouble lately."

Detwiler snorted. "If you call eatin' a cop's face, a tourist's finger, and poundin' your sorry ass into the mud just causing some trouble, then yeah, y'could say that."

"All true, but you have to remember, this is not a highly developed being." Daniel tapped the side of his head. "Think about it from his simple perspective, won't you? He was driven out of his swamp, the only home he's ever known. He was met with violence every time he got spotted on his travels up here. All he's ever known from humans is persecution and abuse. Of course, he's lashing out like a... a mistreated dog."

That slowed Detwiler's sardonic roll. Daniel knew he had a pit bull at home he'd adopted because no one else would. He'd utilized techniques learned from the Wranglers to turn the dog around from alternately cowering or snapping at people to becoming his devoted longtime buddy.

Yeoh remained wary. "We have our orders. The Lizard Man is dangerous, and he has become very high profile. We cannot keep him out of the news, which endangers all cryptids, not just him. You know this, Smith."

Daniel slumped and dropped his hands to his sides. "I know you're right, Jim. But he is the only one of his kind in existence. Can you live with snuffing out such a unique being?

His gaze roved to Detwiler, then back to Yeoh again. "I have an alternative plan if you're willing to help me. We could corral him, toss him in a cage — my Jeep's still rigged up out here — and I could bring him to the Everglades." He took an excited step closer. "Catch and release into an appropriate environment. I'm sure once he's comfortable and free of constant intrusions by tourists, he'll settle back into his former low-profile patterns."

Detwiler shook his head in disbelief. "You must still be concussed," he chortled. "We ain't got jurisdiction in Florida! Besides, what's to stop him runnin' right off that new reservation like he did from Scape Ore?"

"I know a guy—" Daniel began.

Yeoh cut him off. "Daniel, I applaud your kindness in trying to find an alternative so that your charge might live, but what you're suggesting simply isn't viable." He lowered his weapon slightly.

Daniel nodded slowly. Then he gasped and sank to one knee, clutching his midsection. He coughed so hard his shoulders visibly shook.

"Now, see, look at what you gone and done to yourself comin' out here on your fool's errand." Detwiler holstered his tranq gun and went over to him.

"Careful," Yeoh said. He raised his gun again, but now Detwiler blocked his line of fire.

"Of what?" Detwiler scoffed. "Him barfin' on me? The guy's a total mess." He extended an arm toward Smith. "I'll take him back to the MFO so's the chief can cart his sorry ass back to the hos—"

Daniel grabbed Detwiler's forearm in both hands, pivoted, and flung the man ass over teakettle to the ground. Detwiler barely had time to cry out before the air fled his lungs.

Daniel rolled backward and came down with one knee on Detwiler's neck. "Sorry about this." He shrugged. "Even though you're kind of a dick." Then he applied just enough pressure to Detwiler's carotid artery and jugular vein to cut off circulation until he stopped moving.

Daniel immediately slid off to one side, and not just to avoid leaving Detwiler with brain damage. His gaze locked onto Yeoh's tranq gun the instant he heard the soft click of Yeoh pulling the trigger and the whoosh of the cartridge firing. He was able to follow it and easily shifted out of the way before it could hit him.

Before Yeoh could squeeze the trigger again, Daniel launched himself over Detwiler's prone body and sailed across the clearing to land directly in front of him. He backhanded the tranq gun out of Yeoh's hand.

Yeoh immediately dropped into a defensive stance. "Fourth dan in taekwon do, remember? You sure this is a choice you want to make so soon after your apparently miraculous recovery?"

"I sure don't," Daniel said. "What I want is for you to help me. I really mean that." He crouched and rocked back on his heels. "But since that doesn't seem to be an option—"

It was far from as one-sided as his takedown of Detwiler. Yeoh had skill and speed and the confidence born of mastery. He even managed to land a few blows and nearly disabled Daniel by nailing a couple pressure points. Daniel had no doubt that if it were a fight between two equally human beings, Jimmy would have had him at his mercy within a few moves.

Unfortunately for Yeoh, it wasn't.

Without consciously processing all the input flooding in from his senses, Daniel nevertheless found his body reacting with incredible speed and accuracy. His eyes caught every micromovement before Yeoh struck, and instinct took over, enabling him to dodge most blows and block the rest.

Daniel sprang into a forward somersault over Yeoh's head and landed behind him. The startled Wrangler hesitated for a split-second before pivoting. In that instant, Daniel grabbed Yeoh by the upper arms. He swung Yeoh into the air like a toddler and slammed him into the ground. Then he dropped to one knee and wrapped his hands around his throat.

Yeoh grasped his wrists, eyes bulging, and Daniel read the fear in them. He could smell the scent of it rolling off his body, and it stirred something feral deep within. He bared his teeth and snarled. Beneath his hands, Yeoh's neck and face turned a darker shade of red. His feet scrabbled futilely against the ground.

Yeoh's thrashing only made Daniel's heart pump harder with anticipation. But then his horrified rational mind kicked in: Goddamn it, no! He wasn't going to kill an innocent man like some mindless beast. Daniel growled, mustering the shredded remains of his self-control, "Jimmy, please. Don't move."

Whatever Yeoh saw in his expression must have been convincing. He immediately obeyed, releasing his grip on Daniel's wrists and flinging his arms out wide.

Daniel smelled fear coming off him in waves, but the yielding was enough. His instincts accepted the surrender, and although they still urged him to end the encounter brutally and definitively, he was able to deny them.

Breathing heavily, Daniel released his grip on Yeoh's neck and rocked back onto his haunches. "I'm really sorry," he said when he trusted himself to speak again. "I never... this isn't how I want to be."

Yeoh stared at him, gasping and coughing. He said in a voice both raspy and tremulous, "What happened to you?"

Daniel didn't have time to explain. His primary goal still lay ahead, and there were two more Wranglers and two cryptids he still had to handle. Meeting Yeoh's gaze again, he pulled up all his roiling emotions and focused their intensity on him. "If you follow me or try to interfere again, I can't promise you'll survive next time."

Yeoh gaped at him, then scrambled backward until he collided with a thick tree trunk. He wrapped his arms around his knees and pressed against it as though hoping it might open and let him hide within its protective bark.

Daniel stood and sniffed the air. He had the scent of the final Wrangler team and, not far beyond, caught a whiff of the Lizard Man. He also recognized a scent that flooded him with contradictory emotions of kinship and competition. Eva.

He spared Yeoh what he hoped was an apologetic parting glance and then plunged back into the wilderness after his prey.

CHAPTER SEVENTEEN

Eva rolled back, bleeding from the fresh claw marks crisscrossing her chest. She panted, furious that the Lizard Man just wouldn't go down despite the numerous wounds she'd inflicted.

She reconsidered her strategy. Targeting the normally most vulnerable spots along his left side wasn't sufficient. He kept blocking her from ripping out his throat or gouging a vital organ. No, the key was his useless arm itself. If she tore it off entirely, then the shock and blood loss would allow her to get past his defenses and strike a killing blow.

Stan was also exhausted, as much due to the damage sustained before the fight as to the furry fiend's assaults. He needed to end his fun, which was less so now, and finish her off. Unfortunately, his opponent refused to stay still long enough for him to decapitate or tear her heart out. Then he heard something new about to enter their field of combat. Flicking his tongue out, he smelled Unscaled. The damned things seemed to be everywhere, always seeking new ways to ruin Stan's life. He hissed with displeasure.

Eva also caught a whiff of humans. She swiveled her head and spotted two people, male and female, both armed. The male pointed his gun at the Lizard Man while the female took aim at her.

"Nice and easy, there," said the male Wrangler, a brawny fellow who looked like he'd be more at home in a boxing ring. Eva noted that the weapon he had drawn was a large caliber handgun, not a tranquilizer like she'd seen in Daniel's possession.

She shifted her gaze, growling softly at his equally stolid female partner, whose gun was also sizeable and intended for deadly use.

Eva couldn't speak to the Lizard Man any more than he could to her. She also couldn't compel him, having already failed to do so more than once. But she had to communicate her intentions somehow. After all, in their own way, they had gotten to know each other quite well during their extended fight, plus they were both apex predators. And no predator would willingly lie down and submit when the possibility of at least taking their foe with them remained.

Stan's attention was drawn from the bark-hurts in the Unscaled pair's hands back to the mighty cat, who met his gaze with her glowing eyes. She jerked her head ever-so-slightly toward the male Unscaled and then back to the female and flashed her fangs. His heart fluttered as he instinctively grasped her intention and what she expected from him. He slid his nictitating membranes across his eyes in acknowledgment.

In the same instant, they sprang—the cat to her right side at the male and the Lizard Man through the space she'd just occupied at the female.

Screams, then two gunshots, sent a cloud of birds flapping out of their nests in the treetops and squawking through the starlit sky.

CHAPTER EIGHTEEN

Daniel burst into the clearing and found mayhem. He had expected that—just not quite this particular configuration.

Eva had Jarrod Goldman's right arm clamped between her teeth. He was hammering her head with his left fist to no avail. Her middle set of legs pinned him to the ground, and the lower set dug into the earth to keep him immobile. His nine-millimeter lay a few feet away.

Meanwhile, Ella Jackson had her feet jammed against the Lizard Man's gut, barely holding him back as he swiped with his right claws. They grazed her cheek. She cried out but still managed to bring her gun up and point it at his head.

Instinct swept through Daniel, which was fortunate since his intellect had all but seized up assessing what to do first. The Lizard Man was in the greatest peril, so he tackled the huge creature just as Jackson pulled her trigger. The bullet whizzed past the back of Daniel's neck so close he felt its heat, but no damage resulted beyond making his ears ring. He tumbled in a rolling heap of man and Lizard Man, then quickly sprang clear before the cryptid could swipe at him.

A fresh snarl drew Daniel's attention. Goldman had managed to wrap his legs around Eva's waist just below her middle limbs and was boxing the side of her jaw. She reared back and opened her mouth wide, about to cross a line from which there was no return.

Daniel leapt several feet, landed in a crouch beside Goldman, and roared in Eva's face.

He wasn't sure who was more startled by his bestial challenge, but it worked. Eva recoiled and sprang backward off Goldman, tail whipping in a gesture Daniel instinctually recognized as apologetic.

"Jesus effing Christ," Goldman said. He rolled and came up with his gun clasped in both violently shaking hands.

"No!" Daniel kicked the weapon out of his hands, launching it well outside the ring of trees surrounding them. "Stop it, stop this, all of you!"

"Have you lost your ever-loving mind, Smith?" Goldman struggled to his feet, clasping his bleeding arm tightly. "That friggin' catawampus just tried to kill me!"

"If that cat wanted you dead, you'd be dead," Daniel snapped back. "She could've bitten your arm clean off, but she didn't. She just didn't feel like letting you shoot her."

"You talk like that... creature is a person." Goldman's eyes narrowed. "How in the hell are you even standing, let alone fighting?"

"Make sure your partner's okay." Daniel turned to Jackson, who was picking herself up off the ground.

"I'm just fine, thank you very much." Jackson bobbed her head at the Lizard Man. "Can't say the same for your friend there, Smith."

Daniel shifted his attention to the Lizard Man. His charge lay panting on the ground. His now-completely detached left arm lay a couple feet away.

Daniel slapped his hand over his mouth to stifle a cry. The arm must have torn free when they'd rolled across the sward. His maneuver to save the Lizard Man might instead have finished him off.

Eva regarded Daniel with a surge of pride. Her blood had not only healed him, but he'd recovered even faster than a full inductee. He'd also caught up to her and subdued everyone on the field of battle. A part of her still wanted to drive him mewling away from her prey, but another, larger part was honored to yield to this new predator of her own making.

She turned her attention to her original quarry and inhaled his defeat. A pity, really; the Lizard Man had fought well against and with her. But now, the fight had been driven out of him. He groaned in pain, the glow of his red eyes dimming even as they focused on her. She read the plea behind them and crept closer to crouch beside him.

Stan was done. The Unscaled had bested him. He'd lost his arm, and what remained to fight for, really? The opportunity to suffer some fresh indignity, a new source of pain, tomorrow? No, it was time he ended. At least he wouldn't have to wait, shriveling up slowly into darkness. Not when there was someone worthy of ending his misery. He met the great and beautiful cat's gaze and bared his throat to her merciful fangs.

Daniel cried, "Eva, stop!"

"Smith, get the hell away from them!" Jackson started over, but Goldman caught her wrist and pulled her back. "What're you doing, Roddy? He's gonna get himself—"

"Wait," Goldman said. He released her but made a stay-put gesture. "Just... give him a sec."

Eva locked gazes with Danny. Enough of her blood now flowed through him that he should be able to grasp her merciful intent.

Daniel recoiled as a series of images, smells, sounds, and feelings flooded his mind. He realized they were flowing into him from Eva, the same wordless communication he had experienced with Aaron and Willa during his first hunt. He focused until it coalesced into understandability: *The Lizard Man is dying. He wishes me to end his suffering. Would you have me deny him mercy?*

Unsure how to formulate a response her way, Daniel answered aloud. "It isn't that. I don't think he's really dying." He inhaled deeply. "There's no gangrene, even after days of running around with an open wound. No scent of death."

Eva cocked her head to one side, then turned back to the fallen Lizard Man. She leaned closer and sniffed his stump. Daniel was right— there was no decay or fresh blood. In fact, as she examined the wound, she noticed tiny movements within, not of maggots but of tissue almost imperceptibly knitting itself together. She sank onto her haunches and flicked her tail in puzzled acknowledgment.

"See? He isn't dying," Daniel said.

"You sure about that?" Jackson said doubtfully.

Daniel stood and smiled. "We all seem to have forgotten that he's a lizard man. As in, many lizards can regenerate lost limbs. I'll bet he's feeling better now that his dead arm detached, and the process can kick in."

Stan had begun to feel a bit better, physically at least. The constant ache from his dangling arm was gone. Now all he felt was a tingling sensation that he recognized on some level as good. The cat was no longer moving in for the kill, which was also good since he was now less certain he wanted to end.

Goldman smacked his forehead. "Duh, of course... lizard!" He noticed Jackson side-eyeing him and cleared his throat. "I mean, not that it matters, Smith. We have our orders."

"Really?" Daniel boggled at him. "Look at him. He's done fighting. Plus, he can regenerate body parts." He looked from Goldman's blank expression to Jackson's and threw his hands in the air. "Guys, unlike full reptiles, he has the combined physiology of both lizard and human. Don't you realize what that means? His ability to regrow limbs is something the applied bioscience division could study and adapt to benefit humanity. This could be an unprecedented boon to the world!"

"That does kind of change things," Jackson murmured. "But what about the chief's orders?"

"So glad you asked, Jackson." Chief Moore strode into the clearing, her hand resting on the butt of her holstered gun. "My orders remain in full effect." She nodded down at the Lizard Man and then glared at the six-legged mountain lion. "As for her, she's already crossed enough lines playing God with human lives. Remove them both."

"And what about me, Chief?" Daniel stepped in front of the Lizard Man and Eva. "I think it's clear I'm not the same as I was. Am I on your list for elimination too?"

Chief Moore scoffed, "Of course not, Smith. You're still mostly human, and we're not killers like your friends there." She smiled, but her eyes remained cold. "You did attack several of your fellow Wranglers, though, so we will be taking you in for confinement... and since you brought it up, for the bioscience division to perform a thorough examination."

Stan lay observing the scene. He had no idea what all the sounds these Unscaled made meant but sensed they were all more interested in one another than in him. Which was good since he felt too weak to rip off limbs and heads.

On the other hand, Eva understood exactly what everyone was saying and didn't appreciate most of it. It was time to join in the conversation. She rose onto her hind legs and began chanting softly.

"Hey, whoa, what's the cat up to?" Jackson asked, pointing. She, Goldman, Moore, and the newly arrived Samuels watched as Eva Shifted from a six-legged wildcat to a normal four-limbed woman.

"As many times as I've seen her do that remotely, it never becomes less amazing," Samuels said with a note of pride. He pulled off his jacket and held it out, averting his eyes.

Eva sighed as she wrapped it around herself like a strapless shift dress. "You humans and your bizarre morals. All fine 'n' dandy with shootin' me, but," she waved her hands mockingly, "Lo-o-ordy help ya lest y'catch a glimpse of my nethers!"

Jackson snorted but quickly sobered as Chief Moore fixed her with a withering glare.

Eva stepped to Danny's side and patted his back affectionately. "You done good tonight, boy. I might not agree with or understand why you want so bad to save this here scaly booger, but you fought your battles and earned your victory. I, for one, am willin' to relinquish my claim on him, provided you haul his ass outta my territory permanently."

"That's the plan," Daniel said.

"No, it is not." Moore drew her gun and aimed it. A red spot appeared between the Lizard Man's wide-set red eyes. "This creature is far too dangerous to release back into Scape Ore," she shifted her gaze to Daniel, "or any other swamp. Yes, Yeoh told me about your lunatic plan to take him to the Everglades. That's not going to work, even if you could convince Florida to accept him. There's no way to ensure he'd stay put, and next thing we know, he's back to car surfing and attacking people up and down the East Coast.

"As for her." Moore hesitated, then addressed Eva directly. "You don't get to play vigilante anymore, Cat Woman, or steal one more child."

"You got no evidence I done any such things." Eva twisted a lock of hair around her forefinger and gazed up at the brightening sky. Dawn was close to breaking.

Moore sneered. "This isn't a court, in case you failed to notice."

"That's right, we're not a court. We aren't even the police." Daniel folded his arms across his chest. "So, what exactly gives us the right to kill any cryptids? Control them, yes. Confine them, if we must, for their safety and humanity's, sure. But execute them?" He shook his head. "So long as there's an alternative to killing these rare and," he nodded at Eva, "clearly sentient beings, then that's what we should do. Otherwise, we can quit pretending we're on the side of the angels."

Jackson and Goldman exchanged a look. Jackson shrugged. "He's got a point, Chief."

"What was that?" Moore rounded on her, eyebrows arching skyward.

"I mean, that's a woman standing there." Goldman waved at Eva. "I'm not shooting an unarmed woman, whatever she might have been a minute ago."

Lester offered Eva a smile, then stepped between her and Moore, fists planted on his hips. "Yeah, I can't let you do that, Chief. She might be a wampus—" Eva groaned, and he cleared his throat. "Sorry, a cat Shifter, but she started out life human as any of us. She has a job and a house, and a... freaking driver's license! I cannot in good conscience murder her or let anyone else do it regardless of whatever crimes she might have committed."

Daniel jumped in before Moore could respond. "Same goes for the Lizard Man. While he isn't as evolved, he's still self-aware. And now we know he has a regenerative ability that could make him an asset to humanity. Eliminating him means removing all that potential." He smiled briefly. "I'm pretty sure that all goes against the Wranglers' code of ethics and at least one article of our charter."

Moore's expression shifted from self-righteous outrage to uncertainty as her team teetered on the brink of outright mutiny. She lowered her gun but didn't holster it. "What would you all have me do, huh? Just wave away all the violence enacted by these three, send 'em home with a firm talking to?" She fixed her gaze, now pleading, on each Wrangler in turn. "If we release the Lizard Man and he goes on a killing spree, that's on us. And if we ignore what she's done—and don't piss on my leg and tell me it's raining, we all know what that is—how do we face the next kid like you, Smith, and tell him why we let them be stolen and their parent devoured? We have responsibilities, people!"

Silence fell over the group until Eva broke it. "I might can offer a solution to all your problems."

Chief Moore rolled her eyes. "What?"

"Look, I know I can't continue doin'... you know. I've had a good long time in these parts, but maybe it's time for a change. I propose this—y'all return Lizard Man here to his swampy home in South Carolina, and I'll go with him as his guardian."

"What?" Daniel turned to Eva, agog.

"Danny boy, it's for the best. I think I've proven that I'm more'n a match for the big fella, and after tonight I feel like we got to a place of mutual respect." She looked down at the Lizard Man, who flicked his nictitating membranes. Eva winked back. "I'll keep him in the prison that'll make him happiest. And, as an added benefit, I will keep those consarned tourists at bay.

She raised a hand hastily. "Not by eating 'em, I swear. But I'm pretty sure just knowin' a big ol' mountain lion is roaming the area will make 'em think twice about searchin' for our friend here."

"How can we be sure you'll stay put?" Moore demanded.

"Well, I hear there's this secret organization what monitors folks like me," Eva said dryly. "In fact, there's this one fella you already got assigned to South Carolina. I hear he's somewhat competent."

Daniel grinned. "Kind of you to say."

"Smith?" Moore sounded incredulous. "I know you did something to change him into one of you, or something close. How in the hell am I supposed to trust him again with anything, let alone keep you in line?"

"Because he could have done a whole lot worse than he did tonight," Samuels said. "He subdued instead of killed."

"In our case, he arguably saved our lives," Jackson admitted. Goldman nodded in agreement.

Daniel appreciated their votes of confidence but thinking back on how he'd nearly gone too far with Yeoh, even he had doubts. "Look, I'll admit that I've... changed. But I only did what was necessary to preserve lives. If you accept what Eva offers, I swear on my oath as a Wrangler that everyone upholds their ends of the deal."

Chief Moore studied the ground as though seeking its advice. Then she holstered her gun and gave Daniel a curt nod. "All right. Let's try it your way. She—"

"I have a name," Eva said.

Moore rolled her eyes. "Eva takes responsibility for the Lizard Man, and you take responsibility for both." She turned to Samuels. "Afraid that leaves you in need of a new assignment."

He shrugged. "So long as my current one gets a reprieve, I can deal with that." He glanced over at Eva and grinned. She flashed her teeth at him briefly but then looked at Daniel with an expression of, who is this guy?

Daniel chuckled. He did it—he saved the Lizard Man from extinction, and now, thanks to Eva's sacrifice, he could return the creature to the only home he'd ever known. This was worth everything he'd gone through, including whatever he'd become.

The first rays of dawn broke, and Eva's heart broke with them. She didn't want to give up her life, her territory, but knew it was the only way to survive and retain a modicum of freedom. She had made her choices and led her life, and thus had no one to blame save herself.

Besides, how bad could it be? A swamp would have plenty of fresh prey, and if she got bored, she had no doubt South Carolina had its share of seedy criminals to disappear without fuss. The idea of remaining in close contact with Daniel was also less than repulsive. He wasn't fully her kind, so she didn't innately see him as a rival. In fact, she could imagine coming to accept him as something she'd not had in more than a century—family.

As for Stan, all he knew was that no one was attacking him, so he decided to keep still and hope that everyone would just go away while his tingling armhole continued doing whatever it was doing. He rested his head on the ground and closed his eyes as the sun rose, bathing him in its warmth. He didn't even feel the tranquilizer dart because he was already drifting into sweet dreams of rolling around in mounds of plentiful tasty-softs.

ABOUT THE AUTHOR

Hildy Silverman writes in multiple genres, including science fiction, fantasy, horror and blends thereof. In 2020, she joined the Crazy 8 Press authors collective (https://www.crazy8press.com/), which publishes novels and anthologies by its membership. In 2013, her short story, The Six Million Dollar Mermaid, which appeared in the anthology *Mermaids 13: Tales from the Sea* (French, ed.), was a finalist for the WSFA Small Press Award. In 2005, she became the publisher and editor-in-chief of Space and Time Magazine (www.spaceandtimemagazine.com), one of the oldest small press genre magazines still in production, and ran it until 2018. She is a past president of the Garden State Speculative Fiction Writers and a frequent panelist on the science fiction convention circuit. For more information about Hildy, including a complete list of her published work, please visit www.hildysilverman.com.

artist's rendition of the Lizardman of Scape Ore Swamp

LIZARD MAN OF SCAPE ORE SWAMP

ORIGIN: Regional to Browntown and Bishopville, SC, along the edge of the Scape Ore Swamp. Though the recorded accounts begin in the late 1980s, the Creek tribe native to the area tell of encounters much further back.

DESCRIPTION: An aggressive, nocturnal humanoid creature seven feet tall, with green lizard-like skin that is moist and rough, three fingers and toes tipped with long black claws, red eyes, and snake-like scales. In the historic accounts from the Creek, the Lizard Man also possesses a tail. This cryptid is also said to have a craving for butter beans.

HISTORY: The earliest recorded account is from 1929, documenting an older encounter of the local Creek tribe telling of a band of hunters that went out into the night to smoke a bear out of its tree, only the beast that lunged out was a Lizard Man. The hunters scattered, but the creature picked them off one by one, storing their bodies in its tree. When it came for the last of them its attack woke a jaguar sleeping nearby, which attacked the Lizard Man, allowing the last hunter to escape.

The next recorded accounts occurred in the Fall of 1987, mostly of vandalized cars in the area, with deep gouges in the metal like claw marks and chrome looking as if it had been chewed off.

One teenage boy got a flat tire When he stopped to change it something thumped behind him. He jumped into the car when the Lizard Man leapt onto his roof and drove off, swerving to dislodge his attacker. When he arrived home, there were claw marks in his roof and the sideview mirror was torn away.

Over the following months, more reports were made. Local law enforcement ventured into the swamp, discovering long, three-toed prints in the mud, but had no direct encounter with the beast. An airman from the local base claimed to have shot the Lizard Man, providing blood and scale samples as proof, but later retracted his statement saying it was a hoax to perpetuate the local legend. Sighting and damaged vehicles continued to be reported, but dropped off as the weather grew cooler.

In 2015, someone came forth with an alleged photograph and video of the creature. And in 2017, the South Carolina Emergency Management Division issued a warning for residents to use caution during the pending solar eclipse, citing the unusual darkness could trigger Lizard Man activity. Though many discount this cryptid as an urban legend or a hoax, the scientific community continues to conduct research in and around Scape Ore Swamp.

artist's rendition of Catwampus

THE WAMPUS CAT

(Also known as Catawampus, Wampus Beast, Cherokee Death Cat)

ORIGIN: The Wampus is mostly sighted in the Appalachians and the South, but has accounts also hale from Texas, Idaho, Tennessee, West Virginia, the Carolinas, and Washington state. A couple variations of the lore are rooted in native Cherokee legends, but are also attributed to tales told by lumberjacks, likely to keep folk out of the woods.

DESCRIPTION: A nocturnal cat-like creature with an affinity for water, sometimes described as half cat and half dog. It is reported to have glowing yellow or green eyes that can pierce the soul, driving a person insane. It is also said they can start forest fires with no more than their glare, under a full moon. Some call it a water-panther and describe it as black as dusk. It is known for having a loud, terrible voice, but also for being able to change how it sounds to mimic other creatures. Other accounts tell of tufted ears, sharp claws, an unholy stench, and shedding whiskers that are white during the day and black at night. Another defining feature is a right arm like a folding pruning hook, used to snatch prey from the sky, particularly eagles. Depending on the account, it is the size of a Maine Coon, or it stands five feet tall on its hind legs. There are those who say it is bipedal. Others say it has three sets of legs.

In some versions, the Wampus is half-woman, half-cat, with occult powers and shapeshifting abilities. It is said her high-pitched howl is a harbinger of death. When someone hears it, they will lose someone within three days.

There are a lot of wild claims attributed to the Wampus Cat, including curdling sourdough, stealing miners' picks to clean its teeth, marking false trails through the mountains with its claws, and chasing fish from the river by walking through the water.

HISTORY: The Wampus Cat has been blamed for slaughtering livestock since the early 19th century and there have been sightings ever since, generally late at night in rural areas. Some claim she is a witch living alone in the mountains, transforming into the beast to steal chicken and pigs.

There are also two Cherokee legends said to be the origin of Wampus Cat. In the first, a suspicious or curious wife puts on a mountain lion skin to spy on her husband and other men from the tribe as they perform a ritual to prepare for the hunt. When she is discovered, the shaman curses her to live as the Wampus Cat forever, fusing the skin with her flesh. In the other legend a fierce warrior goes out into the night to fight a creature called the Ewah that has terrorized the village. He comes back mad, a mere shell of himself. His wife goes to the shaman for help getting revenge on the creature. They give her a bobcat mask and cover her scent with a black past. When she sneaks up on the Ewah, the sight of her mask turns the creature' magic on itself, banishing it forever. The woman's spirit is said to now inhabit the Wampus Cat as she continues to protect her village.

Hunters are still reporting encounters with the Wampus to this day.

ABOUT THE ARTIST

Although Jason Whitley has worn many creative hats, he is at heart a traditional illustrator and painter. With author James Chambers, Jason collaborates and illustrates the sometimes-prose, sometimes graphic novel, *The Midnight Hour*, which is being collected into one volume by eSpec Books. His and Scott Eckelaert's newspaper comic strip, Sea Urchins, has been collected into four volumes. Along with eSpec Books' Systema Paradoxa series, Jason is working on a crime noir graphic novel. His portrait of Charlotte Hawkins Brown is on display in the Charlotte Hawkins Brown Museum.

CAPTURE THE CRYPTIDS!

Cryptid Crate is a monthly subscription box filled with various cryptozoology and paranormal themed items to wear, display and collect. Expect a carefully curated box filled with creeptastic pieces from indie makers and artisans pertaining to bigfoot, sasquatch, UFOs, ghosts, and other cryptid and mysterious creatures (apparel, decor, media, etc).

http://CryptidCrate.com